The Nightrunners

*#9 in the Edgar Award-winning
Dan Fortune mystery series*

Dennis Lynds

Originally published under the pseudonym Michael Collins

The Nightrunners e-book edition: 978-1-941517-16-1
The Nightrunners POD edition: 978-1-941517-17-8

For inquiries:
Gayle Lynds
P.O. Box 732
125 Forest Avenue
Portland, ME 04101-9998
www.DennisLynds.com

For Margaret Norton

Acclaim for Dennis Lynds & His Novels

"*The Nightrunners* is briskly paced, tersely told." – *The Buffalo Evening News*

"[Lynds] juggles everything around like the expert he is, and the complications are nicely resolved." – *The New York Times*

"A fast-pace thriller … a good book to read at one sitting on a rainy evening." – *Minneapolis Tribune*

"[Lynds] writes with firmness and intelligence. His style is staccato, matched to the action and tone." – *Washington Post*

"Superb characters and excellent plotting." – *Booklist*

"[Lynds] is in splendid form." – *The Detroit News*

"[He] carries on the Hammett-Chandler-Macdonald tradition with skill and finesse." – *Washington Post Book World*

"… powerful writing." – *Library Journal*

"… engrossing and empathic." – *New York Daily News*

"A gripping story." – *The Charlotte Observer*

"Action and intrigue are nicely mixed." – *Publishers Weekly*

"A novelist of power and quality ... one of the major imaginative creators in the crime field." – Ross Macdonald

"Like Ross Macdonald, Michael Collins can write vivid prose and dialogue *and* plot a mystery." – *Ellery Queen Mystery Magazine*

"First-class ... suspenseful, character-rich, and absorbing." – *Kirkus Reviews*

"Some of the rawest, most unencumbered mystery writing extant in the genre." – *American Library Association*

"Tough, believable." – *San Francisco Examiner*

"[Lynds's books are] filled with as much closely observed incident and detail as John O'Hara short stories." – *Wall Street Journal*

"... hot mystery writer whose novels have reached mainstream status. ..." – *San Diego Reporter*

"Collins is the Costa-Gavras of the PI world ... we might also call him the Captain Kirk of PI writers, boldly taking the genre where no colleague has gone before – and doing it so passionately that we can't help but sign on for the quest with him." – literary critic Francis M. Nevins, Jr.

"Lynds is a major contributor to the form, even a redefiner of it; whether or not he is ever given his just due, he should take satisfaction from the fact that he has written mystery novels of genuine distinction." – literary critic Richard Carpenter

Dan Fortune series, by Dennis Lynds, originally published under the pseudonym Michael Collins

Act of Fear, 1967
The Brass Rainbow, 1969
Night of the Toads, 1970
Walk a Black Wind, 1971
Shadow of a Tiger, 1972
The Silent Scream, 1973
Blue Death, 1975
The Blood-Red Dream, 1976
The Nightrunners, 1978
The Slasher, 1980
Freak, 1983
Minnesota Strip, 1987
Red Rosa, 1988
A Dangerous Job, 1989
Chasing Eights, 1990
The Irishman's Horse, 1991
Cassandra In Red, 1992

Paul Shaw series, by Dennis Lynds, originally published under the pseudonym Mark Sadler

The Falling Man, 1970
Here to Die, 1971
Mirror Image, 1972
Circle of Fire, 1973
Touch of Death, 1981
Deadly Innocents, 1986

Kane Jackson series, by Dennis Lynds, originally published under the pseudonym William Arden

A Dark Power, 1968
Deal in Violence, 1969
The Goliath Scheme, 1971

Die to a Distant Drum, 1972
Deadly Legacy, 1973

Buena Costa County series, by Dennis Lynds, originally published under the pseudonym John Crowe
Another Way to Die, 1972
A Touch of Darkness, 1972
Bloodwater, 1974
Crooked Shadows, 1975
When They Kill Your Wife, 1977
Close to Death, 1979

George Malcolm, private detective, by Dennis Lynds, originally published under the pseudonym Carl Dekker
Woman in Marble, 1973

Langford ("Ford") Morgan, ex-soldier, ex-CIA, ex-roustabout, by Dennis Lynds, originally published under the pseudonym Michael Collins
The Cadillac Cowboy, 1995

Other of his works include science fiction novels, literary novels, mystery short stories, literary short stories, short story anthologies, and poetry.

Table of Contents

It was the kind of house that had made my father feel small—a nobody, nothing. Three stories, maybe thirty rooms, and half hidden by its own tall trees on some ten acres of Connecticut woods. A rolled lawn still green in November before the first snow, and a triple garage, with rooms above, that had been a coach house when the country was young. Not the Rockefeller mansion, no, but you knew that the people who lived here were *someone*.

My father had looked at houses like this one and talked about being no one. Not when I was small, but later, just before he disappeared. When I was small he'd been proud of being a New York City cop, but later he watched important men in big cars driving out of big houses and talked about not even existing. People, the world, didn't recognize him as anything. A sense of his life being a waste. Nothing.

I'd taken a taxi from Stamford, and I told the driver to wait as I walked across the lawn to the wide brick terrace of the house, all its windows like glittering eyes in the clear November morning sun. Big houses don't bother me. I think about how free I am—no mortgages, no upkeep, no status to live up to and worry about. I chose my path, and I was glad. You can't be really free *and* really successful in our world. I tell myself all that a lot. Every day.

The maid who opened the door looked at my missing left arm as if she were about to say that they'd given at the office. She didn't say it. Maybe my eyes warned her that I could be more than just another cripple looking for a handout.

"Mr. Wallace Kern," I said.

"He's not in." She started to shut the door in my face.

"He sent for me. Dan Fortune, private detective. You'd better tell him."

She hesitated, and from behind her in the dimness of the big house another voice spoke. A woman's voice, irritable and impatient:

"What is it, Carla? Don't stand there all day."

"A man to see Mr. Kern, ma'am. Says he's a detective."

"Then send him to the office, for God's sake!"

I saw a vague shadow in a distant doorway behind the maid. All in white, with long dark hair. A shape that vanished as the maid informed me that Wallace Kern was at his office—Kern Laboratories. Mr. Kern was, of course, president of Kern Laboratories. When I asked where the hell Kern Laboratories was, the maid looked incredulous that anyone didn't know, and more than a little suspicious of my whole story. She only grudgingly allowed me to wait inside the front door while she wrote down the directions.

■ ■ ■

On the gravel driveway my taxi was gone. Before I could swear more than once, a small red Mercedes pulled up beside me.

"I sent it away," the woman said. "Get in."

She was medium tall, dark haired, not too young, and in a sleek white dress despite the season. The cut of her dress was for her full breasts, narrow waist and round hips, and the color was to show off a fine, unseasonal tan. A mink lay on the seat in case November caught up. Modish thick-soled pumps compensated for legs a shade too short. Her dark hair was long in a smooth flip, and she wore a wedding band. Full-lipped and dark-eyed, she was the woman who had snapped at the maid inside the big house. She drove fast and looked at my empty sleeve.

"You've got a dangerous profession."

"Sometimes."

"What does Wallace want you for?"

"I haven't asked him yet."

"I'm his wife," she said. "Twenty-two years."

She didn't look that old. She knew it, and she wanted me to say it. I hung on as the Mercedes cornered the narrow Connecticut back roads, and let her wait a little.

"You don't look twenty-two years married."

"I'm forty-two. I have a twenty-year-old son. You can tell me what Wallace wants."

"I don't know what he wants, Mrs. Kern."

"Marjorie," she said.

The road came out of the woods in front of a complex of low yellow brick buildings on well-tended grounds. Marjorie Kern drove into the grounds and stopped at the main entrance to the central building. A sign read: Kern Laboratories, Inc.

"When you know, find me," she said. "I'll make it worth your while."

She tossed me a matchbook as I got out. It was from somewhere called The Birch Inn.

* * *

A big, fleshy man, Wallace Kern had neat graying hair and a boyish face. There was nothing boyish about his solemn brown eyes, and his severe gray pinstripe vested suit had "boss" all over it. His rich, carpeted office was furnished with antiques that looked real, and had a view out over the whole plant as if he liked to watch everything that went on.

He stood and held out his hand. He wasn't alone.

"Mr. Fortune." He turned toward the second man. "My executive assistant, Sam Tower. Don't know what I'd have done the last few years without Sam. When my father died, there was no way I could have handled it here without Sam. Production manager here from the start, he had to spoonfeed me the business."

Kern was talking too much. I saw it, and so did the man named Sam Tower. An older man in his sixties, Tower was just under six feet, lean and sharp-eyed. He had the craggy face of an archetypical

New England Yankee, and wore a brown suit that had been carefully cleaned and mended for a lot of years.

"You learned fast, Wally," Tower said. He stared at my empty sleeve. "What do you do, Mr. Fortune?"

"See you later, Sam, okay?" Wallace Kern said.

"Sure," Tower nodded, took a step. "Unless I can help?"

"Just a little private matter," Kern said. "How about those export figures? Maybe by Monday?"

"You'll have them," Tower said.

He left. Not so happy, and still staring at me. Wallace Kern sat down again behind his desk, waved me to a seat. He stared at the door Tower had closed for some time.

"This kind of thing is new for me," he said at last. "I don't want it to get around the company. Sam's something of an old woman, tends to mother hen the whole company."

He was still talking too much, evading his own thoughts. His foot tapped under the desk. He wasn't used to dealing with a private detective, and he didn't like it. He didn't seem to even have noticed my missing arm yet. When he finally got to the point he said it abruptly, like taking medicine.

"I want you to find my brother, Fortune. Bring him home."

"Why?"

He rubbed at his heavy face. "Bill's a gambler. A compulsive. You know how, in the past, men went off on periodical drunks? Sober all year, then binge for a month?"

"The days of demon rum," I nodded. "A decent man wasn't supposed to drink, so if he had to he went somewhere else."

"Bill goes on gambling binges. He goes berserk, vanishes. Consequences don't matter. Nothing matters."

"A paperhanger?"

"What?"

"Does he write bad checks? Con people for cash?"

"Is that what they call it?" Wallace Kern's eyes weren't amused. "Paperhanging. A colorful phrase for cheating and irresponsibility." He sat back, a judge who had passed sentence. "My father always covered the checks, now I do. Perhaps that's a mistake, only encourages him to count on evading retribution."

"The family usually covers. Pros count on *that*."

Kern's nod was resigned. He'd wanted me to know that he wasn't fooling himself, but he was also aware that he'd probably go right on making good for the errant Bill.

"I suppose Bill never found what he wanted to do," Kern said. "Or what he could do. He's seven years older, just missed the Second War. After college my father took him into the company, the way he did me later. But Bill hated it. Since then he's tried all kinds of work. Now he's selling cars, or he was until he disappeared this time."

"You're sure he's gone gambling?"

Kern nodded. "He called Laura, his wife, last Friday from New York—Greenwich Village. He said he was staying with a friend, but he didn't name the friend, and the Village is where most of his runs begin. I know it's only three days, but this time I want to stop him *before* the bad checks start. I need a man who knows New York, got your name from a supplier of ours you worked for once. Here's Bill's picture, a description of what he was wearing, and a retainer check. I've also written down my home and office phone numbers. Call me at any time if you find him."

The photograph showed a tall, lean man with eyes set deep in a long, pale face, and lank hair worn a little ragged. As different as he looked from his well-fed brother, there was a clear family resemblance. There was also a kind of pain or confusion in the deep-set eyes that could be from knowing too little or too much. The eyes of a nightrunner.

I stood to leave, and Wallace Kern finally saw my empty sleeve.

"Your arm! I didn't . . . Are you sure you can handle—?" He stopped. "I'm sorry. It doesn't hamper you?"

I know honest sympathy when I see it, I've seen enough of the other kind.

"Not much. I manage. Where do I find Bill's wife?"

"Seventeen Putnam Street in New Canaan. In a house I own." He shook his head sadly over a man who lived in his brother's house. "But Laura can't tell you anything I haven't."

I headed for the door.

"She's a fine woman, Fortune. Treat her nicely. Not many women today would stand by a man like Bill."

I had nothing to say to that, and at the door I was all but run down by a woman who came in like a high wind. She pushed by without looking at me, and faced Wallace Kern.

"All right, what are you doing about Brad?" she snapped.

No more than twenty-five, she wore a shapeless white smock. Under the smock I sensed a good body, and her face belonged in a beauty contest—an international contest. A brown face, with short black hair, full lips, and blue eyes.

"Anna," Kern snapped back, "I told you—"

They both saw me standing in the open doorway.

"Sorry," I smiled. "Habit of the trade."

Wallace Kern nodded without smiling. The girl looked at me frostily. There wasn't a lot of humor at Kern Laboratories.

I had Wallace Kern's secretary call me a taxi, and went out into the corridor toward the main entrance.

The door to the office directly across the corridor was open. Inside, at a desk, the executive assistant, Sam Tower, sat where he could see the corridor. He was staring at me.

2

On the New Canaan street of white fences and bare November maples, William Kern's house was old and rundown. The small windows and low eaves meant that it had been here when soldiers in Connecticut had worn red coats. It needed paint and repairs, but the garden was neat and the windows clean.

As I got out of my taxi, I saw the low-slung Alfa Romeo parked across the street from William Kern's house. A man sat behind the steering wheel reading. He looked up at me with direct, pale blue eyes, considered me for a moment, then returned to his reading. But I'd seen his face, and it made me stop. There was something familiar about the face.

A healthy face with a firm nose, strong chin and mouth, short reddish-blond hair, and a good athletic color. An uncomplicated face, sure of itself. The face of a rising executive, or army officer, who always knows, right or wrong, what he's going to do next. Vaguely familiar. Not someone I'd ever met, no. Someone I'd seen somewhere. Sometime. A subliminal memory, like a picture flashed briefly on a screen.

I went on to the house. The woman who answered the bell was broad-shouldered in an old ski sweater above brown corduroy jeans, and matched my five-feet-ten.

"Mrs. Kern? I'm Dan Fortune, a private detective your brother-in-law hired to find your husband. Can we talk?"

She turned back into the house without answering. I followed. In a low-ceilinged living room she lit a cigarette.

"Wallace is a good brother," she said. "He worries."

"Don't you?"

"Yes," she said, "I worry."

She sat on a sagging armchair. Her back was stiff. Without makeup, her face was long and angular, but somehow soft despite the prominent bones. The swell of her breasts under the bulky sweater softened her height and square shoulders.

"I worry," she said. "The way a sailor's wife worries. A miner's wife. It's part of my life, and I live with it. He's out there alone somewhere, and I worry, but he always comes back, and I hope he'll come back this time."

Her brown eyes were weary, and I'd heard it before. Too many times. The wives and women of all the nightrunners. Alone and waiting. Hoping.

"Any reason he might not come back this time?" I asked. "Something different this time? A special problem?"

"Not that he told me. Why?"

I moved to the window. "Someone's outside in a car."

She didn't get up. "Yes, he's been watched before, beaten up more than once or twice."

Outside, the Alfa Romeo was gone. That was even more suspicious. Laura Kern leaned back in her armchair.

"Bill was a boxer in college, but he never fights back when they beat him. He says there's no point. If he won he'd lose. They'd only get rougher, and pass the word around so no one would let him gamble anywhere. He says that beating him now and then makes them feel better. They give him more time to pay, and sometimes even consider the debt paid."

I heard the closeness to her wandering husband in her low voice. Two people who clung to each other even when they failed each other. Struggling but together.

"Your brother-in-law says you won't know any more about where Bill is than he does," I said. "I think he's wrong. I think you know a lot more about Bill than he does."

"Do you, Mr. Fortune?"

"If you want him found, I need all the information I can get about where to look."

For a time she smoked in silence. I waited in the small living room. A shabby room, worn and mismatched, but somehow pleasant. The room of people who, for better or worse, have more on their minds than furniture.

"He never says where he gambles, and I never ask," Laura Kern said slowly. "But he's spoken of a Fugazy's Tavern and a Conte's Café, about the people he meets in those places while he waits for what he calls 'the word.' "

"Where a game is," I said. "Okay, I know those places."

"You'll have to show them to me someday." She smiled. "Bill never will. Basically, he's very reserved and proper."

"Most gamblers are. The gambling's their release."

"From the prison of self." She crushed out her cigarette. "Lately he'd been working for Wallace again. Nothing much, some kind of part-time sales, but I suppose Wallace had hopes. Poor Wallace. He likes Bill, but Bill just won't shape up. He always fails the family."

"Speaking of the family," I said, "why would Marjorie Kern worry about her husband hiring a private detective?"

"I don't gossip, Mr. Fortune."

I believed her, and she'd pretty much told me anyway. A little cheating on Wallace Kern, and not exactly a surprise. I thanked Laura Kern, and left. As I reached the door the bell rang, and I opened it on the girl with the pale brown beauty-contest face and short black hair who'd pushed by me in Wallace Kern's office. This time she wore a blue pantsuit that matched her eyes—and pushed past me again. A single-minded girl.

"I want to see Bill," she said to Laura Kern.

"He isn't home, Anna," Laura Kern said lightly. "I don't think you know Mr. Dan Fortune? This is Dr. Anna Botha, Mr. Fortune, a research chemist at Kern Labs. One for women."

"And for youth and beauty," I grinned.

Anna Botha, Ph.D., looked pained, but she also looked me over. There has to be some meaning to male and female. She didn't seem impressed by what she saw—a one-armed middleweight with a lined face of average ugliness and wearing a sloppy blue duffel coat over his only suit, a brown one. A middle-aged roustabout not in her class, and she was one of those bright young women who don't have much time for anyone not in their class or higher.

"Can we talk?" she said to Laura Kern. "Alone?"

"Of course, Anna. I'll make some tea after Mr. Fortune leaves, and cut a cake."

Anna Botha sat down with one leg swinging impatiently. She didn't look very interested in tea and cake, but it was a fine leg.

◼ ◼ ◼

Marjorie Kern sat at the bar of The Birch Inn, the mink draped over the back of her bar stool.

"Well? What does Wallace want you to do?"

"Find his brother and drag him home."

"Oh, hell!"

She drank. Something green and milky.

"Aren't you going to make it worth my while?"

She made a sound that wasn't too friendly, finished her green milk, shouldered the mink, and walked out.

The kind of woman who threw out offers and promises like confetti. Because she never thought about having to keep them.

3

Fugazy's Tavern is on the border between Greenwich Village and Little Italy. A narrow haven out of the November afternoon wind of New York. It was almost empty during working hours, warm and murmuring to the low voices of men who worked at night, or who didn't seem to work at all.

"I should know names?" Tommy Pucci polished glasses in righteous indignation at being asked to remember a transient nonregular by name. "You know how many tourists we get in here, Fortune?"

I showed him the snapshot of William Kern.

"Okay. Faces, okay. Faces I got a million in my head. Sure, that one comes in looking for action. Scotch 'n water, hold the water. Drinks slow, waits long. All night if he got to. Alone, don't talk much. A paperhanger. In here he pays cash up front—no bread, no head. Was in one, no two, days ago. Saturday. Got word on a seat by Cellars's game."

"Thanks, Tommy." I laid a five on the bar. Inflation.

▩ ▩ ▩

". . . big ten, king to the johnny, eight is straight—"

The cards went like bright birds around the green table under the single light. It is always night where Cellars Johnson holds his game, the room as black as Cellars's face outside the cone of light. I straddled a chair behind Cellars.

"William Kern," I said. "White-collar, played Saturday."

Cellars didn't look at me. Neither did anyone else. Real life is serious. Except Detective Sergeant Pine. He looked at me—once. I got the message: he wasn't here. He's a good cop, Pine, and it's a give-and-take world. He'd busted two of his fellow players at other times, and would again if he had to, but poker was his escape, and tonight the game was on.

"Try Fugazy's," Cellars said. "Call ten bucks."

"I came from there."

The cards flew again on wings of hope under the small sun that never set for the players here. Cellars paired his king.

"Two-bits on kings," he said. "There's a woman. White port and blackjack. Makes his breakfast."

"That's all?"

Cellars considered his hole cards. Somebody had raised his kings. He took some time to think, and the raise wasn't all he was thinking about. Naming names can be dangerous, but he knew me when I was sixteen and had two arms, and that rates us as friends. Cellars showed the raiser all his teeth.

"Fifty back at you, friend," and, reluctantly, to me, "Connie Hall, Five-nineteen Hudson."

▓ ▓ ▓

Hudson Street is a wide truck route near the river that shakes to the thunder of heavy tires. Number 519 was a three-story brick flat front over an antique shop.

A woman. I'd liked Laura Kern. I didn't want to find that there was more behind William Kern's bunk this time than bad cards and worse checks. Or was that why I'd been hired, why Wallace Kern was moving fast this time? He'd said that he knew everything Laura Kern did, but did he know more?

Constance Hall had apartment 3-B. The third floor rear, it had a black door with real brass fittings. Brass number, brass knocker, and an engraved brass nameplate—all polished. Constance Hall liked a stylish pad, but she wasn't in it.

"What you gonna do, bang all day?"

A plump young woman lounged in the open doorway of 3-A. She wore a red Japanese kimono, platform scuffs, too much eye shadow, and rollers in her hair. She saw my arm.

"You're her type, all right. She ain't all there neither. Get it?" She laughed. "Just a joke."

"Lost it in the war," I said sadly. "You know Miss Hall?"

"I said it was a joke." Surly, life was always turning on her. "I knows her enough to know you better have a bottle."

I showed Bill Kern's picture. "Does he bring a bottle?"

"The tall one?" She glared at the snapshot as if it were an insult to her. "How does she rate a guy like that? Beat-up bag 'n her 'memories'! What she got to remember? Nothin'!"

"Maybe they remember nothing together."

"Hey," she grinned, "that's good." I'd made a joke. I didn't hate her. "They remembers nothin' together."

"You know when they did it last?"

"Sure, today. Real early today, if you know what I mean."

I left her enjoying her own leer. Downstairs I opened and closed the street door without going out. When I heard her room door close, I gave her a few minutes, then went back up softly and used my keys on the black door of 3-B.

⬛ ⬛ ⬛

Behind the polished brass of the door the apartment was a single room, with a bathroom, kitchenette, dressing alcove, and tiny rooftop terrace opening off it. It was divided into areas for eating, sitting and sleeping, each separate area stuffed with furniture as if Constance Hall had tried to make an elegant townhouse out of a one-room walkup.

The divisions had been emphasized with tall lamps and hanging plants. Too many lamps and too many plants. A jungle, not just dividing but closing off until each section was like a miniature stage set. But it wasn't the divided room, or even all the plants, that made me stare. It was the walls.

13

They were white, but you had to look hard to know that. From floor to ceiling they were covered with photographs and playbills. Glossy eight by ten studio portraits of dramatic male and female faces, action shots of the same face in a series of poses, and candid group pictures of players on stages. All mixed with playbills open to the casts of characters, and covering every wall like some endless wallpaper. Constance Hall's memories?

Mementoes, and not the only ones. As I picked through the plants, and lamps, and cluttered furniture for any lead to Bill Kern, I saw that all the bric-a-brac had been marked as props in some play. The books on rows of shelves were all biographies of actors and actresses, Hollywood confessions, memoirs of the theater, and worn texts on acting. A single-minded woman, Constance Hall, and nothing connected to Bill Kern, not even his name in her address book.

Until I looked into the wastebasket beside her brass fourposter bed. It was a simple note: *Bill, Cebellos expects you at 9 P.M. Be on time.*

■ ■ ■

The dice rolled on the green table, bounced back.

"Seven, a loser."

Hands gathered the bills. The dice passed.

"Try Sal's Garage for the paperhanger. I don' know no Cebellos."

■ ■ ■

In the late night hours he sat in a dark corner away from the table where the cards went around and around.

"You tried Sal's Garage, Rudy's, the Palermo Club?"

"I tried," I said.

He was a big, soft man with a haunted face. No one knew where he lived, if he lived anywhere. He never seemed to sleep, moved from game to game, never played, and knew everyone.

"A nice guy, Kern. Polite. Maybe he got a hotel game."

His name was George. Word said that he worked as a midnight accountant for anyone who wanted shaky books made to look neat. A gentle man who spent his nights watching others gamble and going for coffee. The story was he'd once had a good job somewhere in the Midwest, a wife, and two children. The children had made him afraid. Whenever they had been out of his sight he had imagined every tragedy. He knew he had to let them take risks, live, but he couldn't face what could happen, so he ran away to live alone. Isolated, if anything did happen to them he'd never know it.

"How about someone named Cebellos?" I asked.

"There was a Cebellos was married to Jake Stahl's girl, Danny." His brown eyes hoped he was helping. "Up from Mexico, I think. Flashy young guy. Five-hundred-dollar suits."

The all-night blackjack game was a casino-style operation behind an unmarked door in a midtown health club.

"Kern was around," the dealer said. "Not Cebellos."

On the only table still going, he dealt the cards around to the survivors of the night. Four boozy tourists from some convention, and two quiet professionals—a fat one and a thin one. The dealer flipped his own cards open: ace-six.

"Pay eighteen. Ed pushes. Dutch can't lose tonight. Bad luck, Ohio. Here we go again. No more bets."

"The man wants Nestor, Dutch," the fat professional said. He didn't seem to look at me or at his cards, but he saw both and flicked his down card. He got a nine.

"Nine stands," the dealer intoned. "King bust you, big L.A.? Hang in, you gotta win."

"The man is welcome," the thin professional said, and looked at me with a slow, neutral stare.

A tall older man with blank blue eyes, Jacob "Arizona Dutch" Stahl followed the big action from coast to coast, worked as regular a day as any other professional man, and had never had trouble with the police or anyone else. I'd heard of him, but I'd never met him.

"Cebellos is your son-in-law?" I said.

"Twice, but not any more."

"Twice?"

"Addie married him twice, divorced him twice." His blue eyes watched me without expression. "If your friend is mixed up with Nestor, he'd better count his fingers."

Over six feet tall and bone thin, he had to be sixty and his lined face under thick gray hair showed every year. But in a gray pinstripe vested suit, crisp white shirt, and string tie he sat ramrod straight. Erect, groomed and dignified.

"Maybe she'll stay divorced this time." He gathered his winnings with long fingers. "I never did understand women."

"That's why you got only one daughter," the fat pro said.

I said, "You don't know where I can find Cebellos?"

"The last I heard he was in Mexico."

"Where would I look if he'd come back?"

Stahl studied his new down card. "With Addie it was One-ten Bank Street. Maybe it still is."

░ ░ ░

This late only the entrance was lighted. A renovated brownstone with a brick front. The outer door was open. Nestor Cebellos had an engraved card on the 2-B mailbox. The inner door was locked. My Yale master opened it, and I went up.

I heard voices before I reached the door. One voice, a woman. No one answered the bell, the voice went on talking, and the door was unlocked.

A table lamp made from the statue of a very male nude cast dim light on a garish red, purple and white room. On mirrors, rugs, cushions, and overstuffed couches. On the obscenely male statute, and the nude prints and blowups on the walls. Erotic and gaudy, even lush, but all dirty, neglected and worn out.

Brighter light came from an open bedroom door.

The woman sat on the floor in the gaudy living room. Young and thin in black slacks and a decorated Mexican overblouse that hung to the floor. Her knees were drawn up to her chin, and her long brown hair covered her face as she talked unaware of me.

". . . He'll love me now I'm pretty. . . . We'll go away. He always liked me but my face was too ugly. . . . He'll take me back when he sees me. . . . We'll be fine this time. . . ."

Her voice was almost lost under the tent of her hair. I crossed to the lighted bedroom.

He lay on the bedroom floor. A small young man, slender and swarthy. Dapper in a cocoa-brown suit with a thick silver chain across the vest, silver rings on his small hands, a silver concho belt, and silver-buckled tan shoes.

The pool of blood was dry and black. Shot three times in the chest by a small gun. At least two days ago from the condition of the body, maybe three days.

The girl in the living room went on talking as I called the police.

4

In the glare of every light in the swarming apartment, Nestor Cebellos's garish reds and purples looked even shabbier. The assistant medical examiner worked over the body in the bedroom, and the lab men and precinct detectives spread through all the rooms digging into the private corners of a dead man.

"Three in the heart, I'd say .32-caliber," the ME reported. "Close range, sometime late last Friday or early Saturday."

Lieutenant Marx sat me and the girl on a couch after we'd been searched. She was Adelita Stahl.

"He was my husband," she told them. "He's dead."

"Did you kill him?" Marx said.

"Dutch had a game in Philly," she said. "On Saturday. We went down. I couldn't come to see him until today."

Detective (Second Grade) Leo Puskis came over.

"No gun, Lieutenant. Not inside, not around outside."

Marx nodded. Adelita Stahl went on talking.

"He went to Mexico with that girl. I divorced him again. Dutch said how stupid could I be, so I got the divorce. I fixed my face, he was going to take me back." She smiled at us all. A vague smile, a little puzzled.

"Take her along," Marx said to Puskis. "Find Dutch Stahl, and try to get some story out of them for the last few days."

Puskis took the girl out. She went reluctantly, small and thin and still puzzled.

"No gun on you, Dan?" Marx said.

"You know I never carry a gun."

"What, never?"

"Okay," I said, "you're a music fan. Hardly ever."

"People don't give a cop much time for music," Marx said sadly. "Your case led you to Cebellos, so what—?"

"A job, not a case," I said. "Just finding a missing relative for my client." In a way it was the truth. "Someone said that a man named Cebellos might have talked to my quarry lately. Someone else said that Arizona Dutch Stahl had a son-in-law named Cebellos. Stahl told me that Adelita lived with Cebellos last year on Bank Street. That's it. I came here, found him and her the way I said."

"Does your client and his 'relative' have a name?"

"Not unless, and until, they're in some crime."

"This looks a lot like a crime to me."

"But my client isn't involved."

"His missing 'relative' could be."

"I wouldn't know. I haven't even met him yet."

"How long has he been missing?"

It was a question I'd hoped wouldn't come. A maybe even-money chance, but I'd lost, and I don't lie to the police. In my work, that way lies professional suicide. At least, I lie to them as little as possible.

"Since Friday night," I said.

Marx is a decent cop, he didn't laugh. He didn't even comment. He didn't have to. We both knew that it made my "search" for a missing man more like the "chase" of a runaway. We both knew that Nestor Cebellos had died on Friday night.

"Your client said nothing about Cebellos, and you never heard of him before tonight?"

"Not a whisper," I said.

"What did you find out about him tonight?"

"That he was a big little man in five-hundred-dollar suits, went back and forth to Mexico, was probably a con artist and sharp hustler, and liked mirrors and purple light. What do you have on him?"

"Not a damn thing. Maybe he didn't work in our precinct, or maybe he was very good." Marx looked slowly around the gaudy living room where his men still poked and peered. "The five-hundred-dollar suits are in the bedroom closet—all two of them besides the one he was wearing. And this pad cost someone a bundle—once. The apartment of a man who spent what he made when he made it, Dan. Flush maybe a couple of years ago, but not lately."

"Unless he just hadn't lived here for a while," I said.

Marx thought about that.

▓ ▓ ▓

I thought about Nestor Cebellos, shot to death sometime last Friday night.

Dawn and past on Bank Street, the glow of the November sun already low behind the buildings on Hudson. I lit a cigarette and breathed the sharp morning air as I turned toward Hudson.

I thought about the note in my pocket, *Bill, Cebellos expects you at 9 P.M. Be on time*, and saw Sam Tower across Bank Street.

Sam Tower, assistant to the president, assistant to Wallace Kern, assistant to my client. On Bank Street in Greenwich Village—a long way from Greenwich, Connecticut—at 7:30 A.M. on a working Tuesday.

I walked on without breaking stride, breathing the air as if concerned only with being out in the clear morning after a long night. At Hudson I turned left, flattened against the corner wall, and looked back like an undercover sniper. Tower wasn't on Bank Street, across from Nestor Cebellos's apartment, at that hour, in that place, by coincidence. Either he was following me, had somehow followed the same trail in his own search after William Kern, or had some connection to Nestor Cebellos and knew where he lived.

He wasn't following me. At least, not now.

He stood where I'd seen him, openly on the street crowded with police cars and just beginning to fill with people coming out to go to work. As the city came to life, traffic already jamming on the avenues,

Tower went on watching Cebellos's building as if he didn't care about me, or hadn't seen me.

I cared about him.

An empty cab came up Hudson. I hailed it, and parked him at the corner of Bank. Sam Tower stayed watching for another half an hour. When the last police car had gone, leaving a single patrolman at the downstairs door, Tower left too. He walked to a parked green Toyota with Connecticut plates, got in, and drove toward where I waited in the cab. We followed him around Abingdon Square and up Eighth Avenue.

He stopped at a pharmaceutical supply house on Eighth, and went in carrying two wrapped boxes labeled Kern Laboratories. He came out almost at once without the packages. I guessed that the personal delivery was his cover, his excuse for driving into Manhattan on a weekday morning.

I expected him to turn left when he drove off again, toward the West Side Highway and the route to Connecticut. He didn't. He continued north on Eighth almost to Columbus Circle, and then made a right on Fifty-eighth Street, and parked at the side entrance to the Plaza. I paid my cab, and followed Tower into the hotel.

Inside, he walked the full length of the lobby to the Central Park South side, and came back. He didn't seem to be looking for anyone. He went toward the rest rooms.

A short man in an expensive but rumpled brown chalk stripe reached the men's room door at the same time. They didn't even glance at each other.

Men who arrive at any door at the same time always look at each other. At least a brief smile, a nod.

I went in after them. Inside the outer door I waited for someone to come out through the inner door. I got a good look at the room of white tile, sinks, toilets and urinals. I didn't see Sam Tower or the short man in brown.

I slipped inside. They were nowhere in sight.

Then I saw the two closed toilet doors side by side, a pair of brown shoes visible under one door, black shoes under the other. Neither pair of pants were down.

I almost laughed—the clandestine meeting in the men's room. International intrigue by amateurs.

I took the next booth.

". . . you want to wait a while?" the brown shoes said.

"Something's going on. It might be good," Sam Tower's voice said.

"A detective, eh?" Brown shoes was silent. "Okay, we'll wait. Call me, okay? You leave first."

Through the door gap of my cubicle I saw Sam Tower go. I didn't follow. I wanted a look at the man in the brown suit, and I might have been described. A one-armed man is noticed.

Brown suit waited five minutes. Giving Sam Tower a safe start—I was surprised they hadn't synchronized watches. Whatever they were doing, they were like a pair of clowns taking themselves too seriously. That didn't make them any less dangerous. Men who take themselves too seriously are always dangerous.

When he finally left his cubicle, the short man stopped to wash his hands. The sink faced my cubicle. His back to me, I saw that he was thick and overweight, the expensive suit too tight. But it wasn't an old suit, his handmade shirt was rich, and his tie would have fed me for a week. A man who didn't care how he looked as long as it was expensive, a winner.

In the mirror his fleshy face was beard-shadowed with deep-browed eyes under black hair that had been styled but needed a comb and a wash. He could have been some delicatessen owner, except for his clothes and the eyes. Cold, bright, careful and shrewd eyes. Eyes of power.

When the door closed behind him, I followed. Across the lobby I kept as far back as I could. It's the one time my lost arm is a handicap. He went out the Central Park West side. From inside I watched him cross the street and turn left along the edge of the park. He didn't look back, and I went through the traffic after him.

By the time I reached the statues at the Sixth Avenue entrance to the park he was almost at the Seventh Avenue exit a block ahead.

Sharp and heavy, the point of the knife drew blood from my back under my duffel coat and suit.

"Don't turn. Walk into the park. Smile, look around the trees, talk to me."

An unhurried voice from a tall, wide shadow behind me on the broad New York street that had suddenly become very small, isolated.

⬚ ⬚ ⬚

We stood under the bare trees at the edge of the baseball field where the industrial softball leagues played in summer. The best pitcher I ever saw pitched here one summer for W. R. Grace. The MONY batters couldn't touch him, swore he was a ringer.

"Can I stop talking now?" I said.

I'd talked and smiled at nothing all the way along the path beside the park drive to the deserted diamonds. I hadn't tried to see him. The knife was still a needle in my back.

"You can start." His slow voice was neither menacing nor nervous. Steady, with no breath wasted. "Who are you?"

"Dan Fortune. A private investigator."

"Who are the two men you were tailing?"

"The one in the brown suit I don't know. The tall old guy is a Sam Tower. He works for a company called Kern Labs."

Behind me, he was silent for a time.

"Did you kill Cebellos?"

"He was killed Friday. I got there this morning."

"When did the girl get there?"

"I don't know. She was there when I found the body."

In another silence, sweat poured down under my shirt with the trickle of blood from the knife point.

"What took you to Cebellos's place?"

"Following a lead on a job."

"What job?"

"Looking for a man named William Kern. His brother hired me to find him."

Again silence, his thinking as unhurried as his voice.

"Shit."

His arm came around my throat. A muscular arm that pulled me back against a broad chest and the sharp knife point. An arm that tightened like the steel collar of a garotte.

Blood hammered in my ears. Purple and green clouded and exploded in my eyes. Consciousness slipped away down a plunging slide into darkness. Moving on its own, detached, my lone arm clawed back at an ear, a thick neck. . . .

I never lost consciousness all the way.

Blind, deaf from the roar in my ears, suspended by the neck without air, I swam in thick shadows. Felt myself sat down against a tree. Limp, strangled . . . floating . . . sick . . .

The light, and the park, and the tree I sat against returned in waves of nausea. I was alone. People, men, moved through the park in the November sun. There was no way to tell which of them carried a hidden knife.

After a time I got up and left the park to catch a passing taxi and ride down to my one-room loft on Twenty-second Street.

◾ ◾ ◾

I slept ten hours.

When I climbed out of bed it was dark again. In my "bedroom" separated from my "office" by only a table, I dressed in jeans and a sweatshirt, took my suit and duffel coat and went out to have the knife slits repaired and get something to eat. I'd lost a whole day, but I wasn't ready to start after Bill Kern again. What had he gotten into? What had I?

I went to a movie. One of those smash-hit, mindless violent adventure flicks about a gang that was going to blow up Alaska, or

Peru, or somewhere. I don't remember because halfway through I had a vision. It didn't matter, nothing real was going to happen in that movie anyway.

A vision of two pieces of paper.

Back in my office-apartment I laid them out side by side—the note I'd found in Constance Hall's apartment that told Bill Kern to meet Nestor Cebellos, and the memo of information about Bill that Wallace Kern had written for me.

The handwriting was identical.

5

I leaned across the big desk straight into Wallace Kern's round prep-school-boy face.

"You knew Cebellos was dead."

The train from Grand Central had dropped me in Stamford at 8:36 A.M. Wallace Kern let me cool my heels in his outer office until 9:20 while his secretary pretended to be very busy at her typewriter. Sam Tower's office was empty when I passed, and no one came into Kern's office while I waited. The big, graying president smiled when he finally let me in, but I wiped the smile off with my blast.

"You hired me to 'discover' him dead and call the cops so you'd be all innocent and surprised!"

I dropped the two notes on the desk under his nose.

"The same handwriting—*your* writing. You sent brother Bill to meet Nestor Cebellos on Friday. Start the whole story from the beginning."

His face grew red and his eyes darkened. "I don't like being told—"

"I can have the cops of two states crawling all over you in an hour!"

He stared at me. He shifted his bulk in the desk chair. Then he bent to his intercom.

"Ask Tom Craig to come here."

He sat back but he didn't relax. His fleshy fingers drummed on his desk. His eyes were uneasy, not looking at me. Distant eyes, troubled. He looked toward the door behind me as it opened and closed.

"You wanted to see me?"

I turned. It was the man I'd seen in the Alfa Romeo in front of Laura Kern's house. A shade under six feet, he was slim and trim with good shoulders and a narrow waist in denim riding jeans under an open white lab coat. A classic light-heavyweight—with the reddish-blond hair and healthy face that had been somehow familiar to me. It still was. A colleague?

"What did you do," I said to Wallace Kern, "hire two of us?"

"Two of you?" Wallace Kern sounded confused.

"I saw him sitting in a car outside your brother's house Monday morning."

The man, Craig, smiled. "That would make me a pretty poor detective, Fortune, wouldn't it?"

"Then what were you doing there?"

"Trying to be sure that Bill didn't slip in and out again without contacting Wallace. He's done that in the past."

Wallace Kern said, "Dr. Craig is our vice-president and chief of research. A good friend who's helping me."

"Who hasn't helped much so far," Craig said.

The research vice-president had an easy voice, calm and direct. As uncomplicated as his face. But underneath I heard an earnestness like a thin steel wire. A man who needed, and got, results. The modern young executive in his casual jeans under the long lab coat, doing his job without concern for irrelevant trivia like the team uniform or a status home in the proper suburb.

"Where do I know you from?" I said. "Somewhere."

"Perhaps the magazines," he said lightly. "Or the newspapers a few years ago."

Newspapers. Yes! Over two years ago. Craig. *Dr. Tom Craig.* The Battling Schweitzer of Bolivia. The American doctor aboard a jetliner that crashed in the Bolivian jungle, and who led the survivors out to safety, treating their injuries all the way with not much more than aspirin and a pocket knife. The doctor who then remained for over a year at a remote medical station in the heart of that jungle ravaged by the government's war on the remnants of Che Guevara's rebels. Took charge and turned that advance station into a hospital that treated rebels, government soldiers, and the bewildered Indians caught between. Stood up to both sides, with a stethoscope in one hand and a rifle in the other.

"*Time* and *Newsweek*, yes," I said. "That was some act."

"Ancient history," Tom Craig said. "Yesterday."

Wallace Kern wasn't having that much modesty. "About as heroic as a man can be, Fortune. He had a broken arm when he led those survivors out to the station, and he didn't lose one of the seventy-two. He wasn't even a practicing physician. Our assistant research chief then, and we'd sent him down to Bolivia on a straight business trip. When he got the survivors out he could have come home a hero right then, but he stayed. He made that miserable little station into a real hospital, and battled and treated everyone who needed help in that tortured country."

"I was there, Wally, what else would anyone do?" Craig said in his easy voice. "After the crash we all had to try to get out alive, I had the skills."

"You didn't have to stay down there," Kern said.

"They needed a hospital with that guerilla war going on. I saw that the station could be made into one. So I did it."

"Not everyone would have, or could have," I said.

Craig shrugged again. "I could and did. But that's the past, Fortune, we've got the present to handle. In a way, my adventure down there led to Wally's problem."

Wallace Kern nodded unhappily. His voice was nervous and angry at the same time.

"It's my son, Fortune. Brad's in a Mexican jail. He has been for three months, and will be for fourteen more years! Fifteen years in some Mexican hellhole!"

"Mexican? That's how Nestor Cebellos came into it?"

Wallace Kern nodded, but didn't go on. He brushed at his eyes, and swiveled heavily around in his chair to look out the window behind him. Tom Craig took over.

"Brad was convicted on some drug charge, we haven't even been able to get the details. Probably at least half a put-up job, I know Latin countries. Brad never used any drugs. About a month ago Nestor Cebellos showed up and offered to help."

Wallace Kern turned. "We tried every legal action. We exhausted every option of the Mexican legal extortion system! The American Embassy says it can do nothing!"

"What about the prisoner exchange? Can't you get him out on that? They're sending most drug cases back to the States."

"Not Brad! Not eligible they say—because of all our legal efforts. His papers are all tied up!"

"Pretty much a stone wall," Tom Craig said. "Then his brother Bill brought Cebellos to Wally. Bill met Cebellos through the daughter of a gambler he knows. Cebellos nosed around in Mexico, and told Bill he might be able to help us."

Wallace Kern shook his head. "This kind of thing doesn't happen to people like us!"

"It does when you have kids," I said.

"Wally didn't know what to do," Craig said, "asked me to help. I've got important work here, but I know that world and speak Spanish. Wally isn't used to dealing with men like Cebellos."

"How was Cebellos going to help?"

"By bribery!" Wallace Kern said angrily. "He said he had the contacts. Filth and corruption!"

"But it had the ring of truth and reality," Tom Craig said drily. "He said he could at least make things easier for Brad, and maybe even get him out. I told Wally to give him some money, and see what results we got."

"How much money?"

"Five thousand for a start, plus three thousand up front for Cebellos," Craig said. "Two weeks ago we got word that Brad could receive packages—and had been moved from a prison deep inside Mexico to the minimum-security jail in Piedras Negras just across the border from Eagle Pass, Texas."

"Results," I said.

"Yes," Craig agreed. "Last week Cebellos contacted Bill, told him that the move to Piedras Negras was part of a plan, and that for another five thousand, and three more for him, he could get Brad released."

There was a silence in the office. Wallace Kern was looking out the window again. At his multimillion-dollar plant, and the workers moving between the buildings. Dr. Tom Craig studied his fingernails. I watched them both.

"You sent Bill to Cebellos on Friday night," I said. "With eight thousand dollars."

"Yes," Wallace Kern said.

"No wonder you wanted to find him fast this time."

"When Bill called Laura on Friday night," Craig said, "he said nothing about Cebellos or the money. We waited all day Saturday. Neither Bill nor Cebellos contacted us. Cebellos had an unlisted number, so I went to his apartment."

"And found him dead."

Craig nodded.

"Alone? No gun around? Nothing that tied to Bill?"

"Alone when I found him, I saw no gun, and I didn't remove any evidence." Craig continued to study his fingers. "We didn't want to reveal ourselves, and we had to find Bill. So I told Wally to hire you. We hoped you might find Bill and the money without our connection coming out."

I said, "What time Friday night did Bill call his wife?"

"After midnight," Craig said. "Almost one A.M."

I let it just hang there. Three or four hours after Bill had been supposed to meet Nestor Cebellos, and exactly the hours in which Cebellos could have been killed.

"Who could have killed Cebellos?" Wallace Kern said, turned to face me. "Why? What does it mean for Brad?"

"Maybe nothing," I said. "To a gambler eight thousand dollars is a lot of money."

"No!" Wallace Kern said. "Bill wouldn't kill anyone!"

"But he might run with eight thousand," Tom Craig said. "Or get killed himself for eight thousand in that world."

He was a practical man.

"Unless Cebellos's hustling caught up with him," I said. "Bribing for favors and advantages can cut two ways. You can step on toes, get in other people's way."

"You think Bill and Brad could be caught in the middle of something?"

Wallace Kern stared at both of us. His boyish face seemed to reflect the graying of his hair.

"So cool? So impersonal? We're talking about my son! My brother!"

"We'll help them, or we won't," Craig said in that calm voice. "Blowing our tops won't do anything, Wally."

"Damn your logic!" Kern said. He turned to me. "Find my brother, Fortune, and find out what happened to Cebellos. Find out what it means for my son!"

6

She walked ahead of me in the sun. Dr. Anna Botha. Her intense young face was a clear brown in the crisp morning light, but I had a hunch she would call herself black these days. She wore a slim gray skirt this time, a short brown corduroy car coat, and strode toward a blue Chevy.

"Going near Stamford?" I said.

"Why not?"

So she wanted to talk to me. That was fine, I wanted to talk to her.

"You know Brad Kern pretty well?" I asked as she drove us out of the parking lot and turned east.

"You heard me ask Mr. Kern about him, didn't you?"

"What was he doing about Brad, yes," I said. "What is Kern doing about Brad?"

"Are you going to pump me, Mr. Fortune?"

"Yes."

She pulled off the road and stopped on the shoulder near a wide white gate in the shadows of a grove of old Connecticut oaks. There were horses in the field beyond, and a large white house with barns across the field. Green, neat and rich.

"What are you doing for Mr. Kern?"

"A trade-off?"

"All right. I'm engaged to Bradley Kern. More important, I like him and know him as well as anyone. There is no way in the world that he could do anything criminal."

"And I'm a private detective hired by Wallace Kern to find his brother Bill."

She waited. "That's all?"

"That's it," I said. I felt a little guilty of cheating on the trade-off. I needn't have. Anna Botha could take care of her own interests.

"Did you find Bill?"

"Not yet," I said. "Why did Brad go to Mexico?"

She watched me in the car, and I wondered about her. Wallace Kern hadn't mentioned her, and he hadn't said anything about her connection to Brad. He hadn't mentioned Sam Tower either. When I left the big president's office Sam Tower's office across the corridor had still been empty. The assistant to Wallace Kern seemed to keep his own hours. Maybe Wallace Kern just didn't think Tower or Anna Botha were important.

"So?" The blue eyes studied me from her rich brown beauty-contest face. "Bill isn't just on one of his gambling binges?"

"I can't say for sure. He could be."

"No. Something else." Her bright eyes seemed to peel me. "He may be gambling now, but he wasn't. Something for Mr. Kern. About Bradley."

"Okay, yes. That far I can go, but no further unless you can show me you already know the rest."

She leaned her slim back against the car door, her small, firm breasts rising under the car coat, and thought. Close to me, her looks held up even with her mind on something else. Most women, or men for that, tend to lose some of the dazzle in their looks when you get close, see each feature separately. Not Anna Botha. If anything, she seemed better looking. And as she had been talking I'd begun to hear a faint accent. Almost imperceptible, but there. A kind of British-Colonial intonation, maybe the West Indies, but just about gone.

"All I know," she said at last, "is that Bradley went to Mexico for what he said might be a week or two. After only a week he was arrested on some kind of drug charge, and sentenced to fifteen years! I know that Mr. Kern and Tom Craig are trying to get him released. I know that I haven't seen or heard of very damned much in the way of results!"

"Do you know a Nestor Cebellos?"

"No."

The answer was quick, but not evasive. Brushed off as if I were changing the subject, being irrelevant. As if it never occurred to her that I was still talking about Brad Kern.

"Brad went to Mexico on vacation?" I asked. "Alone?"

"You mean without his fiancé? An engaged man."

"That's what I mean."

In the field the horses had grazed toward us. A magnificent chestnut put its head over the fence and watched us curiously. A thoroughbred with soft, empty eyes.

Anna Botha looked at the horse. "I was born in South Africa. In Capetown. Do you know what a 'Colored' is in South Africa?"

"Part black, part white," I said. "In every European colony, but special in South Africa. Until recently they made a big distinction down there between blacks and Coloreds."

She nodded. "You must read a lot."

"I was a sailor, and I live alone."

"Three groups not two," she said, "with the Coloreds more European than native, feeling very separate from the blacks. Before the Boer War one of our leaders tried to establish a separate Colored nation in the north away from the Afrikaners and the tribal blacks. It didn't work out too well, so most of my people lived in Capetown, closer to whites, and with many privileges blacks didn't have. Until recent years."

She went on watching the horse at the fence. "When we lost many of our privileges, were lumped more with the natives, my family left South Africa. I've lived in this country over fifteen years now. I left South Africa, but not our cause. We're more black now, and I work for human rights. For the people of my homeland, yes, but I want to see all people become human beings, the end of the exploitation of the few by the many."

Now she looked at me. "Bradley thinks the same way I do. He wants to do something. Young as he is, he's a serious man despite the money, the family status, and his mother."

"You don't think he went to Mexico on a vacation. You think he went down there with a purpose."

"If it was a vacation, he would at least have told me he was going. He didn't tell me."

A statement and a question. She had more on her mind.

"You're afraid he could be guilty. At least technically," I said. "His father and Tom Craig were quick to tell me that Brad never used drugs. You haven't even mentioned it. You don't think it matters whether he used drugs or not."

She moved from where she had been leaning on the door, and slid around behind the steering wheel again.

"I better get you to Stamford. I'm late now."

She started the car and pulled back onto the road. Her narrow skirt had hiked above her knees when she moved. A skirt four inches above the knee on smooth thighs is more physically exciting than a string bikini.

"If I'm going to try to help Brad, Anna, I've got to know everything I can."

"*Doctor* Botha," she said. Her small nostrils flared.

"Sorry."

She glanced at me as she drove. A searching glance.

"All right, I'm sorry too. Call it female reflex these days. An educated female. And black."

"And young, and beautiful."

"Yes," she said. "Are you really going to help Bradley? Try to get him released?"

"If I can."

She drove. "One night a few days before he went to Mexico, he was tense and nervous. I asked him what it was. He said he couldn't tell me, but that I'd like it. That's all, except for one offhand remark later that night—for once Kern Labs was going to do some real good even if they didn't know it. At the time I was thinking about other things and let it pass."

"Now?"

"Now I think he had some kind of medical help plan on his mind. In Mexico. What else do we have at Kern besides medical products?" Her eyes flickered toward me. "In other words, Mr. Fortune, drugs."

"Dan," I said. "You think he was carrying medicines, drugs, and the Mexicans couldn't tell the difference?"

"Sometimes there isn't any difference, Dan, except the intended use. Morphine, for example."

I thought about that. "Morphine could be very valuable in Mexico. To the wrong people."

We were in the outskirts of Stamford, traffic growing.

"You sound as if you have a reason to think that," Anna Botha said. "The wrong people, and Bradley."

"Maybe I do, and I don't think I'm the only one. I've got a hunch that vice-president of yours, Tom Craig, is worried about the same thing. Brad in the middle of something."

"Tom's usually right. A little too competitive, the superstar, but he faces facts. What he did down there in Bolivia was no surprise to us at Kern Labs."

"You like Craig?"

"I admire him, so does Brad. He does what he says he will."

"How about Wallace Kern and his brother?"

She smiled. "Mr. Kern's too conservative and a little narrow, but he always means well. There's still a lot of the all-American boy in him, and he grew up on business. Brad and I try to open his eyes to the world. He even listens. Bill?" She picked her words. "Bill's a perpetual failure trying to hide from himself and telling himself that the world failed him. Brad likes him, but I don't have much use for his kind. He's basically just lazy, no use to anyone." The harshness of the young, vigorous, and successful.

"And you don't think much of Mrs. Kern? Marjorie?"

"There's nothing to think much of. The misery of the world is less important to Marjorie than her convenience. No, I'm wrong. She doesn't know there is a world beyond her convenience. All she knows is herself, and not even that, really. She just acts. Whatever she feels at the moment."

"She seems interested in what I'm doing."

"Does she?"

"Could she be trying to help Brad too?"

"She might stumble around, if she happened to think about Brad." We'd reached the Stamford station, and she parked and leaned against the door again, her face turned to me. "Where does Bill fit in, Dan? He does, doesn't he?"

"He brought a man to Wallace Kern who said he could help get Brad released. Kern gave the man money, and he got Brad a transfer to a smaller Mexican jail close to the border. He said it was part of a plan to get Brad out, but he needed more money. They sent Bill to him with the money on Friday. Now Bill's missing, and so is the money."

"Nestor Cebellos? That's the man who offered to help?"

She hadn't missed the name after all. I'd remember that.

"Yes."

"Has something happened to Cebellos?"

"He's dead. Shot late last Friday. I only found him dead on Monday."

"But not Bill or the money?"

"No."

She watched the few people waiting on the train platform in the bright November sun. "Bill will gamble away every dime he gets, and do almost anything to get it."

I had nothing to add to that.

7

She was in the bedroom, bent over the bed with a knife in her hand like Medea over her children.

When I came up the stairs at 110 Bank Street this time, I heard not voices but noises. Angry noise, with furniture banging and drawers slamming. There was no police seal on the door of Nestor Cebellos's apartment, and it wasn't even closed.

The gaudy living room had been torn apart. Literally. Red and purple was ripped, slashed and strewn like blood among the wooden bones of flung furniture. The noise came from the bedroom. I saw the woman with the knife.

She stabbed the upturned box spring as I watched, and dug into the cloth and springs, swearing in Spanish.

A short, sturdy woman with heavy breasts and muscular legs. Her purple dress was open almost to the bottom of her vast cleft. An ordinary dress, tight at the top and flowing wide over her hips and thighs. Sandals on her feet—huaraches. She looked like a peasant who should have been far from New York. Curved and full but not heavy, and all her parts fitted together. The kind of peasant woman who once made kings dally when they were supposed to be out hunting.

"Find it?" I said.

She whirled, the knife up. The reflex of a cat, a jaguar. Of a woman who has learned to protect herself at all times. Not scared, but ready. She looked at me for less than a second, and went back to her search. The reaction had been pure reflex, she didn't care who I was, or who saw her searching the rooms.

"Get out of here."

She had an accent, swore in Spanish, and her face was a dark-skinned oval with heavy black eyes under jet black hair. A haughty nose and full lips. The eyes faintly Oriental. High cheekbones. Amerindian somewhere not too far back. Mexico, or south. The face smooth and clear and no more than eighteen to twenty-five. It was hard to be more definite. The kind of girl who matures early.

"Let's look for it together," I said.

She moved to the closets. The bureaus and desk and night table had already been searched.

"The police are going to want to know who you are, what you want here," I said.

"Are you the cops?"

"No."

She went on pulling the $500 suits from the closets.

"The money or the gun?" I said. "Or something else?"

On her knees she crawled around the closets.

"You know he had a wife," I said.

She stretched up to the closet shelves.

"Did she know about you?" I said.

Out in the bedroom she brushed the dirt of the apartment from her skirt, and her angry eyes probed for anywhere she might have missed. Then she walked past me into the living room and on out the front door.

I walked slowly around the wrecked red and purple living room. And the bare little kitchen. She hadn't missed that. I'd come to see if the $8000 might still be somewhere in the apartment. If it was, and she hadn't found it, no one was going to without tearing down the walls and raising the floors.

The woman came back. She didn't have her knife, but she did have two men with her. One was Lieutenant Marx.

"Gazzo wants to talk, Dan."

I knew why there had been no police seal on the door. They had left it clear to see who might come calling.

■ ■ ■

Captain Gazzo had been my mother's lover.

That was a long time ago, after my father left the NYPD and went wherever unimportant men who can't stand being unimportant go. It's a bond between us, but it gets me no favors, so I cooled my heels in his outer office while he talked to the woman.

(Maybe the past does get me a shade extra benefit of the doubt at bad times. He knows me, and he's human. But, then, he gives everyone the benefit of any doubt he can find.)

The woman came out on her own. She gave me only a quick glance as she passed, but I had the feeling that she'd know me again even in a crowd. I went in to Gazzo.

"What were you doing in the apartment? You told Marx your client had no connection to Cebellos."

Gazzo was behind his littered desk in the dim light of drawn shades. He says that in his work it is always midnight anyway. The deep furrows of his face are like a steel engraving, and his gray eyes hadn't slept. There are those who say he has nowhere to sleep: no home and no bed. I know he has insomnia—the occupational hazard of a good policeman.

"He does now," I said, and told him about Bradley Kern. "I went to see if the money was still anywhere around that apartment. Did you find any money?"

He shook his head. "If the paperhanger had it, maybe it never got to Cebellos. That could be why he was killed. He didn't have the money, and someone figured a double-cross."

I said, "Why does it rate your rank to investigate?"

Gazzo rubbed the thick gray stubble on his seamed face. He needed a shave. He usually did unless he had to wear his gold braid for some ceremony. Sixteen years ago he took acid in the face, and his skin is tender.

"What do you know about Nestor Cebellos, Dan?"

"Nothing more than I've told."

In the dim office, the captain's eyes turned inward as if seeing all the dead young fools looking for the easy path to the big score. The story of his life: every way of death there is; every violence of the half-sane mind of man. He'll have to retire soon, and he used to say what the hell would he do if he retired? He hasn't said that lately. His voice was slow.

"Cebellos was a Mexican national, so we reported it all to Immigration. The Chief got a call from Washington. Border Patrol. It turns out that Cebellos was one of their prime informers. You know how it works: an informer gets a percentage of everything recovered when he turns up a smuggler. A nice game, especially when the informer is a smuggler himself, and Border suspects Cebellos was. All sides for a peso, turn in your rivals for fun and profit."

Another nightrunner. Of a different kind.

"He sounds like a busy boy," I said.

"Very busy." Gazzo rubbed at his stubble. "We ran his prints all around. Four years ago he was a security man at an L.A. department store. He and his wife tried to shake down a man accused of possessing stuff stolen from the store, offered to withhold evidence for a price. The man turned them in. They slipped through the charge on a technicality, but Cebellos got deported."

"His wife? Adelita Stahl?"

Gazzo nodded. "LAPD thinks she never knew what was going on, did what Cebellos told her. After he was deported she divorced him. Border Patrol helped him get back into the country, and eighteen months ago he was suspected in a con game right here. The scheme misfired, Cebellos ran to Mexico before he was picked up, and there was no solid evidence—except against his wife."

"Adelita again? She'd remarried him?"

"She swore Nestor was clean so he was never charged. She got a year's probation and another divorce."

"Now?"

"We don't know. He'd been working with Border again, but they were suspicious of smuggling. He must have gotten wind, and moved back up here some six weeks ago. About a month ago he started making trips down to Mexico. He stayed away from Border, and had another guy with him. No line yet on the other guy, and the Mexican cops say they have nothing against him."

"Maybe he bribed the right people."

Gazzo sat silent and gloomy in the dim office.

"Who's the woman Marx brought in with me?"

"Luz Cebellos, his sister. His only relative, and a U.S. citizen. His stuff is hers now, she went to see what it was."

"That's her story for tearing up the place?"

"Looking for hidden valuables. It could be true, Dan."

"Did you find the gun? Get a make on it?"

"The ME says probably small, lightweight, and short-barreled. A pocket or purse gun. No trace of it yet."

"What did you find out from Adelita Stahl?"

Gazzo had once appeared on one of those TV talk shows. The MC had asked what was the worst part of dealing with criminals. That they have families like everyone else, Gazzo had said.

"That he was going to take her back and marry her for keeps because she'd had an operation on her face and was a lot prettier now." The captain glared at the wall. "She was in Philadelphia over the weekend with Dutch Stahl, came back on Monday and went to see Cebellos. She found him dead."

"When did she go to Philly?"

"Early Saturday." Gazzo poked at some papers on his desk. "Friday night she was in their hotel room with Dutch. He had a game about eleven P.M., left her alone. No one around the hotel saw her leave that night. She says she didn't."

* * *

Wrought-iron lions flanked the two-step entrance. A narrow, carpeted lobby had a single elevator at the rear. Potted green plants, an odor of scrubbed cleanliness, and a desk clerk who still wore a black suit, dark tie, and starched white shirt. The Marquis Arms.

One of the small residential hotels off Lexington in the Twenties whose "guests" have lived there or come there for years. Middle-class and sedate.

"Mr. Jacob Stahl? Who shall I say?"

"Mr. Daniel Fortune."

The clerk nodded solemnly and disappeared. Privacy and manners were important at the Marquis Arms. Neither rich nor elegant, even a little shabby to keep costs down for its clientele, the hotel was a solid oasis in a flimsy world of Hyatts, Hiltons and Holiday Inns. The people who moved through the tiny lobby weren't rich or elegant either, and had the same sense of quiet solidity and manners.

"Go right up, Mr. Fortune. Seven-H."

On the elevator I wondered if the Marquis Arms knew how Arizona Dutch Stahl made his living. When the tall old gambler opened the door of 7-H, I realized that it wouldn't matter. Tall in soft charcoal-brown flannel, his dignified face looked like that of some veteran church deacon under his neat gray hair, and his long hands were clean and reserved. He looked as conservative as the people in the lobby, maybe more so.

"Come in, Fortune."

Across the old-fashioned room Adelita sat almost as I had first seen her. On a couch near the windows, with her feet out of sight under a wide skirt, and her knees up to her chin. Her head up this time, the long straight hair combed and pulled back, she was looking out the windows, silent and motionless.

"You stay here often?" I asked Stahl.

"Thirty years, when I'm in New York. I work in the big hotels and clubs, I don't have to live in them. Here it's quiet, comfortable, and you get decent service."

He was as conservative as he looked, a small businessman at heart. Something inside had made him different, and he lived in smoky rooms and casinos, worked the late and silent hours, ate in restaurants, and made his home in a hundred hotels, but I could see him sitting quiet and proper while the drunks and swingers swirled frantically around him.

"Adelita lives here with you?"

"Sometimes. She doesn't like hotels much. Her mother didn't either. Women like houses. Private prisons." His blue eyes considered me. "You didn't come to talk about hotels."

"What can you tell me about Nestor Cebellos?"

He sat down. "What's your interest in Nestor?"

"My client was doing some business with him. William Kern was the go-between, with money. The business is hanging, the money is missing, and so is Bill Kern."

He thought about that. He had spent a lot of years being careful to think before he moved or spoke.

"I can't tell you much. In my business you mind your own hand. I play cards. I don't roll dice, bet on horses, or do business where Cebellos did. He was a flashy hustler with cons, schemes and fast footwork. He didn't score often, and like all second-raters he remembered the scores and forgot the misses."

"How did Adelita find him?"

"Through me. She wanted him, married him, gave him everything she had or could get. I'm not sorry he's dead."

"Any ideas why or who?"

"Anything he did, anyone he knew."

"Did you know he was an informer for the Border Patrol? Probably a smuggler himself, too?"

"No, but don't look for surprise. Anything for a dollar except work or violence. Danger wasn't his line."

"A double cross?"

"If I had to bet, I'd say his hand got out too far."

"Or in the wrong pocket?" I said. "Can I talk to Adelita?"

Stahl looked toward his daughter. She had turned on the couch, and with her hair drawn back I could see her face now. A thin face, as delicate-boned as her body. Oval and pretty with small, regular features. Nothing stood out except the dark shadow of her eyes that looked as if she hadn't slept in years, a pinkness to her skin, and some small scars at the hairline.

"You're the man in the room where Nestor—" Her voice shook. A low voice, withdrawn. "I remember you now. I didn't know. . . . I guess I was a little crazy. We were going to get married again. When his job was over. We—"

"Addie—" Stahl tried to break in.

"No," she said. "Don't tell me anything, Dutch. He told me. He was tired of running, of trouble. He was going to get a stake and start a business in Mexico. We'd be fine."

"Adelita?" I said. "What job did he mean?"

"Something he had to go to Mexico for. A real job. When he was paid over the weekend we were going to Mexico. Both of us. So on Monday—" Her low voice went lower. "I found him."

"Did you find any money?"

"No. I don't think I looked."

"You were alone here all Friday night?"

"Dutch had a game. I took a bath, watched TV, and went to bed. We had to go down to Philly early Saturday."

"She was asleep when I got home," Dutch Stahl's voice was stiff and curt, angry. "Ask about my alibi. I was in a game, but it was in the Village not far from Bank Street. Everyone leaves the table sometime. The john, a drink, or maybe to get some air. No one in a game really knows who goes or for how long. They all swear I never left, but they don't know for sure. Maybe I shot him!"

"Maybe," I said. "I'm not sure I'd care except that it would clear my client and his affairs. I'm more interested in Cebellos's job, anything he said about it."

"He didn't say anything," Adelita said. She got up. "I'm going out, Dutch. Don't wait for me for dinner."

She took an old cloth coat from a closet.

"Nestor had a sister," I said. "Where does she live?"

"Luz," she said, "they didn't get along. Out in Jamaica. New York Boulevard, 2670 I think. Near that anyway."

Her small hands in the coat pockets, she left. Jacob Stahl watched her go. His ramrod back sagged under his suit.

"She's twenty-eight," he said. "Fifteen when her mother remarried and she came to live with me. She was a shy girl, no confidence, no good in school, but with something she wanted an awful lot way down inside. I don't know what, I don't think she ever really did. Something. She was twenty-two when she met Cebellos. She's pretty, but she never believed that. When she was a kid an accident left scars on her face. You could hardly see them, but she was sure they made her ugly. If she was beautiful everything would be perfect. She had three operations on her face, the last only six months ago."

"Maybe she'll be better now."

He was silent. "Anything else you want, Fortune?"

"Where would I find Bill Kern when he's got money?"

"Too many places." He looked at me with those flat eyes. "This money, is it a lot?"

"Enough."

"Kern got it from your client to give to Cebellos?"

"Yes," I said. "What's on your mind?"

"A paperhanger like Bill Kern would do plenty for a good stake. Cebellos would try any hustle. A nice team."

"You're saying that the whole thing could be a scheme? Cebellos and Bill cooked it up to rip off my client?"

Stahl shrugged. Bill Kern and Cebellos in a con game to bilk Wallace Kern? There never was any plan to help Bradley Kern rotting down there in a Mexican jail?

8

I looked the other way.

Six of them ringed the well-dressed man against garbage cans ahead in the fading light.

I looked at the house numbers.

I hoped that Luz Cebellos lived at 2670. You don't ask questions about people in the 103rd Precinct. Not if you're white and a stranger. Not in Jamaica. Not this year.

The encircled man ahead was tall and thin in the dusk, and what the hell was he doing on New York Boulevard? He had no damn right to be here, in need of help, among the prostitutes and the idle who waited for another day to end. Where the silent couples and bitter youths stared into store windows at what they couldn't have, and two stray boys with bloated bellies sat on the curb of the gutter eating imitation ice cream sundaes from paper cups because when you have nothing you must have something.

The six young toughs ahead had hate. Black and brown, thin-assed and small-balled in tight pants, they taunted the older man who should never have been there. Bizarre in capes, fur jackets, purple and yellow and lavender shirts, high-heeled boots and fantastic hats. Wide-brimmed hats and hats without brims; decorated hats and hats cut out in designs. Rings on their fingers, and chains hanging down. Flamboyant, because when you are no one you must be someone.

"Hey, old man, you lookin' for a broad?"

"Naw, he just come to help us poor folks."

Their voices were loud in the twilight. I walked closer. And before I reached them I knew—the house where they menaced the man at bay was the house I wanted. Their violence blocked me, the restless energy that had nowhere to go in Jamaica, but had to go somewhere so went into the violence they lived with. Boys who still knew death, who had seen brothers die young.

"You ain't scared of us, old man, is you?"

I had nowhere else to look, nowhere left on the darkening street to be neutral, and I heard the cornered man's voice.

"Punks don't scare me! Get out of my way!"

I saw his face in the dimness—Sam Tower! Gaunt and alone, the special assistant to Wallace Kern defied them. Sweat stood out on his Yankee face, but anger raged in his voice.

"Scum! I'm warning you! The police—"

I pushed through them to stand beside him against the garbage cans.

"Well lookie there!"

"We got big trouble now! One 'n a half!"

They were all gristle, and we were an old man and a cripple, but two is more than one, and I was an unknown. It made them reassess their position, and lose their moment.

"The man!"

The other world of Jamaica arrived. A patrol car that came slowly along the boulevard. Sam Tower was fierce.

"Now you damned punks, you—!"

He spoke to no one. As silent as shadows in the dusk the six youths were gone. In Jamaica the police are the enemy, *them*. The soldiers of an occupying power, storm troopers. And on the twilight street Sam Tower and I stood alone as the patrol passed on the deserted boulevard and moved on.

"You have a car?" I asked.

Tower pointed to the next block of shops and lights. I hurried him to the car, got in beside him. When he reached to start the engine, I stopped him.

"I've got business. What are you doing here?"

"That's not your business."

"Of course it is. Your boss hired me. Did he send you?"

"No."

"On your own? Why? What are you doing?"

Tower looked out at the now dark street, his face stern as he watched the passing blacks as if they were mysterious aliens.

"Wallace is involved in something. I worked with Mr. Kern senior for twenty-five years, for the company thirty years. I have a right to worry about Mr. Kern's son and his company."

"You think Wallace or the company is in trouble?"

"Why did he hire you? Who was that Nestor Cebellos?"

"I was hired to find Bill Kern. Anything else you want to know you'd better ask Wallace Kern."

"William?" Tower's face showed distaste. "A total failure, useless to the company. He was a great sorrow to Mr. Kern."

"You thought a lot of Mr. Kern senior?"

"He was a fine man. A great man."

"And you intend to protect his son and his company? Which one comes first? Son or company?"

"I know my duty, Fortune."

"How does the man at the Plaza fit your duty?"

"What man?"

"You met a man in a brown suit in the men's room."

"No, I did not."

"I tailed you from Cebellos's place. I saw you." I didn't add that I'd heard them too. It's best to keep a small edge.

"He's a friend, personal business. Stay out of my affairs, Fortune, they don't concern you."

"I hope they don't, but the only reason you could have for being here is Luz Cebellos, and that concerns me. What did you want with her, and what did she tell you?"

"I want nothing except to protect our company, and the woman wouldn't talk to me. She wouldn't even open the door!"

"What did you think she could tell you?"

"If I knew that I wouldn't have to talk to her." Tower started the car. "I'm tired, I'm going home now."

I walked back to 2670, slow and watchful. The six toughs didn't reappear, and no one else looked at me twice. I didn't belong here anymore than Sam Tower did, but my old duffel coat, black beret, and empty sleeve fitted better. It's strangers who are the enemy everywhere.

Number 2670 had been the typical Queens middle-class blue-collar two-family house with a postage stamp front lawn and driveways on both sides. Now the lawn was a square of bare dirt, the paint had peeled, and the windows were patched with cardboard or covered inside by blankets. Luz Cebellos had the left half of the house. I rang. Her voice—some female voice—came from a distance, " . . . *tell you . . . beat it?*"

"Miss Cebellos? It's Dan Fortune! I was picked up with you at Bank Street!" I called it to the silent house. To the dark night. "Can we talk?"

I waited alone on the night steps.

The door opened.

There was no light inside, and no one stood in the black opening. Only silence as I stepped inside.

■ ■ ■

She lay in bed in the second-floor room, her black hair thick and loose on her pale brown shoulders, and her Indian eyes on me. The shadows of a single hanging bulb picked out her high nose and full lips. She had three men with her. One of them was in the bed.

He was a skinny Latin with a hairless chest, a little pencil mustache, and glistening brushed hair. He looked like a dandy, but muscular biceps with corded veins said that he made his living lifting something heavy. He had one arm around Luz Cebellos, possessive. His other hand held a long cigar. He smoked it with a kind of arrogance.

"How'd you lose the wing, *amigo?*" He pointed the elegant cigar at me, and fondled Luz Cebellos under the sheet.

"Shot down over Tokyo, *amigo.* "

The second man spoke in Spanish to Luz Cebellos. He sat across the room in a broken-down armchair. Short, thick, with a pale round face dark with beard stubble, his hair was gray and a black mustache swept down below his mouth like the stereotype of a Mexican bandit. His Spanish had the sound of a question.

The third man was the one who had opened the door below, and followed me silently up to the second-floor bedroom. Now he sat on the arm of an old couch behind me. Small, thin and clean shaven, he had a swarthy face with large, feverish eyes. He said nothing.

I said, "Can we talk alone, Miss Cebellos?"

"Man, where's your manners?" the dandy in the bed said. "You're lucky we's even holdin' off a while, you know?"

The mustachioed one in the chair said something again. Guttural Spanish, with a coarse accent I didn't know.

"They're friends," Luz Cebellos said. "What have we got to talk about, mister?"

"Who killed your brother, maybe."

The bandit mustache spoke again. Luz Cebellos answered in Spanish as she went on watching me.

"What do you care?"

"Nestor was supposed to be doing a job for my client. He got paid, but he didn't finish. We want to know why."

"What kind of job?"

"I was going to ask you that."

She shook her head. The muscled dandy in the bed was busy with his hands under the sheet. She pushed him away without looking at him.

"Nestor never talked to me about his business, or about anything else," she said. "Who knows who killed him?"

"Or cares, Miss Cebellos?"

From the bed, one smooth dark hand holding the sheet halfway up the rise of her breasts, she considered me. Her peasant face had no expression, only the gleam of the dark eyes.

"That too, yes. Why not? What good was he? A big, empty wind who lived on his own delusions. Useless alive or dead. At least there's one less for my parents in Mexico to bleed for. One less to bleed *them* dry. He only went home to hide. No, Mr.—whatever your name is—I don't think I care very much who killed Nestor."

She looked like a peasant, and until now she had seemed to act like a peasant, but as she spoke more than a single sentence she didn't sound like a peasant. English with polish and vocabulary. Somehow, somewhere, she'd been educated.

"Or why?" I said.

"Or why."

The gray-haired man's Spanish was a sharp grunt this time. Luz Cebellos's Spanish was a lot smoother, almost Castilian to my ear, and I suddenly sensed that she was translating for the older man. Not everything, but some of my English that the man didn't follow. A man who knew some English, but not too much.

"Could Adelita have shot him?" I said.

"Maybe. She loved him enough."

"Is that a motive? Loving him?"

"Be a woman in our world and you'll know. Any world for that matter," she said. "It could be a motive if your man was Nestor Cebellos."

"Then it could be a motive for Dutch Stahl too."

"Why not?"

"Or anyone Nestor knew or worked with?"

"You sound as if you knew Nestor."

"No, but I'm being filled in," I said. I wasn't getting very far. Somehow, I had to get some reaction from her, or maybe from all of them. "All I know so far is that Nestor was supposed to be helping my client to get his son released from a Mexican prison. He'd come to my client with the offer to help, got paid, and got some results. So my client sent him more money on Friday night, and Nestor got shot."

The lover in the bed said, "Money?"

"Nestor offered to help?" Luz Cebellos said. "His idea?"

"That's how I hear it. A rip-off, maybe?"

"With Nestor I'd believe it."

The dandy said, "How much money?"

"Eight thousand first, eight more on Friday."

The dandy sat up in the bed, letting the sheets drop. Luz Cebellos's full breasts swung exposed like tropical fruits. I seemed to be the only one who noticed.

"Baby?" the dandy said.

"Don't drool, lover. I didn't find any money."

"You wouldn't hold out on me?" the dandy said.

"Don't push it, honey. It's not your business."

Her tone had the sting of a slap. The dandy reddened as much as a brown face can. He took her face in his hands.

"Hey, baby, you gotta be nicer, right?"

The other two men came alert. They didn't have to. In the bed the skinny one went suddenly rigid. Under the sheet, Luz Cebellos's hand had moved. It stopped five inches from the dandy's hidden belly. There was something in the hand. Something she pressed against his belly. His hands dropped from her face, and his voice was almost a squeak.

"Hey, only kiddin'! I got all I want, right baby?"

There was scorn in her voice. "All you can handle."

"Sure, baby, sure." Sweat oiled his face.

I said, "The money you do care about?"

"Why not? What else is there to care about? Who killed him? I'll let you care about that. You and the police."

"How did you know about the money?"

The older man's Spanish was rapid-fire. He was on his feet—short, solid and bowlegged. Luz Cebellos took some time answering him. He didn't sit down, stood watchful.

"I didn't know about the money," she said to me. "But he was shot for something, and with Nestor that usually meant something valuable. So I looked. You know what I found."

"And you don't have even a guess who shot him?"

"No."

"Okay, if you think of something, call me."

I turned to the door. The smaller, hot-eyed one who hadn't said a word stood in front of it. I stopped. Behind me, the older one growled his Spanish.

"Give me your address and phone number," Luz Cebellos said.

"Two-ninety-eight West Twenty-second Street. The phone's 993-0071."

"We'll talk about price if I call," she said.

The smaller man moved away from the door.

9

A man can't hide in a small town. Not from others, not from himself. So he comes to the city. From ancient Babylon to New York now, the pursued and the lost have come to the city to hide. From the hunters outside, or the hunter inside.

Only the city is my land, and if I am the hunter sooner or later I will find my rabbit. I know how to hunt through the solitary rooms and the faceless river of humanity, through the forest of stone and the glare of neon, through the shadows and the silence. But I didn't find Bill Kern.

Not for the rest of that night, or the next day, and by late afternoon I had begun to think that my quarry and the missing money were no longer in the city.

A thin November rain had begun to mist the high buildings and slick the gray streets as I returned to my own office-apartment hide-away to regroup.

A car was parked at the curb in front of my door. A small red Mercedes with its motor running. The window slid down.

"I'll buy you a drink."

Marjorie Kern smiled at me. A bright smile, like the sun breaking through the gray drizzle.

In the dim, carpeted cocktail lounge she looked even younger than she had in Connecticut. Younger and softer, carrying a feeling of sunlight with her in the deserted lounge.

"I always liked it here. Do you like it, Dan?"

"I like it," I said.

The small lounge of the Henri Cinq on West Twelfth Street, quiet, plush and rich. I liked it, if I couldn't afford it most of the time. Did she know that?

"I don't think you like me very much, though. Or I don't think you did when we met. I'd like to change that. Can I?"

She smiled again. It was a soft smile. Not a sexy smile, enticing. The opposite. A clean bright smile full of life. Honest, and it curled my toes. I carry more than my share of the bruises we all get from the adversary system we call love between the sexes in this country, and enticing, calculated smiles don't get far with me anymore. Her smile did. Person to person. Was I wrong about her?

"You want me to like you?"

"Yes, I do."

The long, dark hair that framed her well-kept face caught the muted light of the lounge. She wore a white blouse and a youthful gray suit. A gray tweed storm coat with fur at the collar and sleeves, and high-heeled black boots that rose to meet the slim skirt, made her look like a girl ready to play in the snow. Almost a different woman, the sense of sun that she had brought into the lounge coming from inside. As if something had changed inside her, or had changed for her.

"Why?" I said.

"Because I need you."

An offer after all? Another promise she had no thought of having to keep? Maybe she wasn't any different.

"For what?"

She looked down at her scotch and water. A simple drink this time. Her smile faded.

"I had a long talk with Anna last night, Dan."

"Anna Botha?"

She nodded. "You know she's in love with my son. Now she's worried about him, even scared. So am I. I realize that Wallace hired you to find Bill, but I want you to help Bradley. I—"

"It looks like the two things are the same."

Her dark eyes blinked at me. "How, Dan? I mean, I don't under-stand what it's all about."

"Neither do I yet."

"But you'll find out, and you'll help Bradley. For me. You'll tell me everything that happens. Will you, Dan?"

"You want me to report to you as well as to your husband?"

"Yes."

"Doesn't your husband talk to you?"

"I'm not sure he thinks I care." She poked a manicured finger at the ice in her scotch. "I haven't been the best of mothers. I'm self-centered, I admit that. I don't want to be old, I'm not ready to be the mother of a grown man. I don't want to just sit and watch. Perhaps it's not the most wonderful way to be, but it's the way I am. Only I *am a* mother too, and my son is in trouble."

"He has been for months."

"I know. I didn't think. . . ." She drank. A long drink. "Last night Anna said that she didn't believe Bradley went to Mexico just on a vacation. I don't either. He's a serious boy like his father, but more intense, idealistic. Not at all like me. Why did he go down there? What happened? I have to know, Dan, and I'm not sure Wallace can handle it." She drank again, emptied the glass. "Anna and I don't think he would have gone just on his own. We think there has to be someone else. Someone who went with him, or sent him."

"Your husband?" I said.

"Perhaps. I . . . I'm not sure. I can't think why, but—?"

"Nestor Cebellos? Bill Kern?"

"I don't know." She waved to the waiter for two more drinks. "But why is Bill hiding if he doesn't know something? He's a weak man, easily led and easily scared. He could be afraid to tell what he's done or what he knows."

"He's a gambler. He could be just on a binge."

The waiter brought the drinks. She drank quickly, automatically, and her face changed again. Soft and loose, with deep and distant eyes.

"I want to know, Dan. I don't trust Wallace in something like this. I need someone stronger. A man who knows the awful world Bradley is caught in." She looked at me, her eyes steady and almost naked. "I always have needed a man like that."

It was oblique, like some ten-year-old sidling up and offering me his sister. The hint that she needed more from me than help. Was I reading my own suspicions into her words? Or had I been wrong about her earlier? I'd seen her as a woman who had no interest in a man like me, who liked only the rich and the powerful. Did I look powerful to her? Strong? We never really know how others see us. Or maybe all she wanted was someone to lean on for the moment.

"I can pay you, Dan," she said.

"No," I said.

"I don't mean money. I know Wallace hired you. I mean a trade. I can give you some help."

"What help?"

"I spoke to Laura, too. She'd heard from Bill. He called her this morning. He sounded terrible, even despondent. Laura is very worried this time."

"Where did he call from?"

"Here in New York. Some midtown hotel with a poker game he'd been in before. He said he had a room at the hotel."

"Come on."

She paid the check. We drove back to my office-apartment. In the darkening mist of the November drizzle she clung to my arm. Ever since Delila. Or was it only a woman who didn't want to be the mother of a grown man but had to try?

Whichever, her grip on my lone arm did the damage.

They were in the downstairs hall. Three of them. Two had automatic rifles, and my arm was held.

■ ■ ■

The hot-eyed, clean-shaven one leaned on the wall near my door, his automatic rifle short-barreled and ready. The gray-haired older man with the bandit mustache sat at my desk, his rifle in his lap. Luz Cebellos stood in front of us.

"Don't move," she said, unsmiling. "They're dangerous. From South America somewhere. Rebel guerillas."

We sat on my two straight dining table chairs. Marjorie Kern stared at Luz, at the two men. I watched Luz.

"What do they want?

"I'm not sure," Luz said.

The older gunman growled Spanish. Luz nodded without looking at him.

"You're with them," I said.

"They've been watching your place all day." Cool and calm, her back to the older gunman. "They walked in on me yesterday, I couldn't stop them. It's Nestor, whatever he was doing. They want to know who he was involved with."

The younger gunman at the door let out angry Spanish. The older one nodded, hesitated a moment.

"Woman." He searched his mind. "Say what we tell, *si?* Say . . . tell . . ." He gave up and went to Spanish.

Luz turned to Marjorie Kern.

"What does Cebellos do for your husband?" She was translating the gunman's Spanish word for word. She went on without any change of inflection. "Answer them. Don't resist. They're in a war, and in enemy territory. They're dangerous and nervous, you understand? Answer fast and easy, look cooperative. Don't try to fight them."

I suddenly saw that she was playing a dangerous game. She was with them, but not for them. While she acted as their voice in English, she was trying to help us by telling what she knew and warning Marjorie Kern. A risky game, hanging on an edge. Their English was bad, but how bad? How much could she get away with? Marjorie Kern wasn't any help.

"No! They don't scare me. This is America! Who do they—!"

The older gunman snapped Spanish. Luz answered. Her voice was toneless, like a parrot. The gunman pointed at Marjorie.

"Woman." Pointed at himself, "Man." Raised his rifle, "Gun." Pointed at Marjorie, "No gun."

She stood up. "I won't stay here to be threatened! I don't have to."

"Sit down!" Luz said. "They mean—!"

The young one pushed Luz aside. He took Marjorie by the shoulders and flung her back down into the chair. The older one began to snap questions. Luz translated rapidly.

"Cebellos was with your husband. Who else was there?"

"Ask him! Are you afraid to threaten a man?"

"Who sent the boy to Mexico?"

"Bradley? What do you know about Bradley?"

"Where did the boy get the drugs?"

"Bradley never used drugs! I'm calling the police!"

The gray-haired gunman came around the desk quickly. He stood over Marjorie looking down at her.

"*Policia?*"

Her eyes were wide and defiant. Angry—and very bright as she looked up at the menacing gunman. Shining eyes, luminous. She looked at his face, at his thick hands that held the rifle, at his broad chest, and I sensed an excitement. A thrill inside her. He was a ruthless man. A violent male. And she was defying him, fighting him. A scene from a thousand Hollywood movies—the defiant heroine and the fierce hero. The lady and the pirate, the queen and the outlaw. A fantasy—taken by the violent male. A fantasy she probably played with every man. But this wasn't her bedroom or the late show.

"*Policia? Stupido!*"

She spat in the gunman's face.

"Ahhhh . . . !"

The younger gunman jumped forward, his rifle up. He grinned. He had small, broken teeth. He aimed the rifle straight at Marjorie and squeezed the trigger. The long burst shattered the room and riddled my ceiling as the older one knocked the gun up.

Marjorie blinked.

I sat rigid.

The older gunman wiped his face. He stared at Marjorie, and shook his head with a kind of wonder. I guessed what he was thinking—she wasn't brave, only ignorant. So ignorant of their world that she didn't believe any threat, couldn't comprehend the danger, didn't know enough to be afraid. The gunman said something in Spanish.

The young one leaned his rifle against a wall, and punched Marjorie in the face. She screamed. Chair and all, she went over in a heap, blood oozing from her mouth.

I stood up. The older gunman poked me with his rifle. I sat down. Luz Cebellos was expressionless. Marjorie swayed to her feet. The young one hit her again. Blood spurted from her nose. She fell. The young gunman bent over her.

"No! No!" She covered her face with her hands, curled up knees to chin. Her gray suit was stained with blood, and her black underpants were grotesque above her boots and bare legs.

The older one nodded. The young one took her by an arm, and dragged her across the floor to my bed. He lifted her to the bed, took her hands from her face, and slapped her hard. She screamed. He slapped her again.

The older one began to talk. Luz translated.

"Nestor Cebellos was a jackal, a murderer."

The young one hit Marjorie.

"The boy in Mexico is a murderer."

The young one ripped her blouse down the front. Her breasts quivered exposed, full and high and tight.

"Cebellos deserved to die."

The young one began to take off his shirt.

"Who sent the boy to Mexico?"

She huddled on the bed. "I don't know! Please. I don't know what Bradley was doing! Please, please. . . ."

"Who else works with Cebellos and the boy?"

The young one reached to touch her naked breasts.

"Please, please." She didn't look at the gunmen, or at the hands that touched her. She was crying. "Please . . . don't. . . . Don't touch me . . . please . . . don't. . . ."

Crying on the bed, she begged them, all her defiance gone. The real thing was no fun, no thrill.

"She doesn't know anything," I said. Luz translated. "She doesn't even know what I do, and I've told you all I know. We don't know what the boy was doing, if he was doing anything!"

They both looked at me. Luz said something in Spanish. They both looked at her, and then at me again. They . . .

Feet came up the stairs outside. A knocking on my door.

"Fortune? Open up! Captain wants to see you downstairs."

Both gunmen swung to the door, rifles ready.

"Five minutes! Then I'll come and get you!"

The feet went down the stairs. The gunmen looked at Luz. In her rapid Spanish I caught one word: *policia*. The gunmen held a quick debate. The young one buttoned his shirt, the older one spoke to Luz.

"They'll go now—this time. Don't try to follow, or to warn the police," Luz translated, and in the same tone, "They believe you for now. Do what they say, or it'll be bloody."

"You?"

"I go with them."

They went out carefully, Luz in the lead. I jumped to the door and locked it. I turned to help Marjorie, but she was already sitting up. Wide-eyed, like a frightened bird.

"They're gone," I said. "We're okay. Can I—?"

She looked down at her bare breasts and exposed thighs. She buttoned her torn blouse, pulled her skirt down.

"Animals! Pigs! I'll . . . I'll . . ."

"Easy now," I said. "I'll—"

"You? What did you do? A man? You're a man?"

"Sorry," I said drily. "Next time I'll eat their guns."

"You call yourself a man? You let them—"

Her courage came back fast, or her fantasy. In an hour she wouldn't remember that she'd been afraid. It was already my fault, and I wasn't getting that clean bright smile now. I let her rage while I waited for the police to return. They didn't come. I began to feel uneasy.

"You better get away from here," I said.

She stopped her raging. "Leave? You mean, alone—!"

"I'll take you down to your car."

I went first. The stairs were deserted, and the street was quiet and empty in the dark and drizzle. When she saw no danger, she strode past me to her parked car. Her voice carried back:

"They'll wish they never heard of me! I promise you!"

In the Mercedes she screeched away. She took the corner into the avenue on two wheels, and a taxi driver screamed curses. She ignored him, asserting her power. The Mercedes vanished.

I went back into my building. I hadn't been wrong about her. By tomorrow she'd have the whole incident rewritten in her mind into the triumph of the defiant heroine. A world of one. Then what did she really want with me?

I closed my office door.

Dr. Tom Craig sat behind my desk. He held a heavy steel rod.

10

"You were lucky," Craig said.

Neither a joke nor a warning. A statement of fact. In a dark blue suit that hung nicely on his slim frame, Craig swiveled in my desk chair. Unhurried, but with a shine to his pale blue eyes like an athlete waiting for the game to begin, or waiting for his turn in a game already begun.

"Where did you come from?"

"Out on your stairs. The floor above."

I guessed that his eyes had shined the same way when he brought those crash survivors out of the jungle, when he made that jungle station into a hospital. As if action brought him to life. A job to be done, and under his shock of reddish hair he smiled. The confident smile of a man of action who has already started to act, and I knew why the police hadn't returned.

"It was you," I said. "That knocking on the door."

He nodded. "I saw Marjorie's car outside. I'm the curious type. I heard enough through the door to get the picture. A nasty pair. Cebellos must have gotten in their way."

"You think they killed him?"

"Can't be sure." He was careful with his opinion. "It sounded like it, and they'd kill like swatting flies."

"Your act was a big risk, then. If they'd felt trapped, they could have exploded on us."

"A risk," Craig agreed, "but a good one. They seemed to be trained, but not professionals. Idealists with a stake in their future, and obviously still after someone or something. They weren't getting any help from you or Marjorie, and I didn't think they would want to attract attention before they got what they wanted."

He considered it like the scientist he was, cool and objective. "I estimated that they were trained enough not to panic easily, and involved in their cause enough not to want an open battle or a man-hunt before they found what they were after. I calculated that if I made them think the police could show up any moment, they would pull out without shooting and wait for a better time."

"Pretty close figuring," I said. I thought, but didn't say—with our necks.

"I couldn't see what else to do, and something had to be done fast," he said earnestly, as if really worried that there might have been a safer action. "That Luz Cebellos seemed to be trying to help you, so I thought it worth the try."

"You could have called the police."

He shook his head. "That *was* a bad risk. Those two are the emotional kind, unpredictable. Sirens might really have panicked them, and a police siege would have left them no way out. A sure blood bath. I gave them a chance to pull out unseen, and the time to do it in."

"Neat and logical." I nodded at the steel rod in his hand. "But what were you going to do with that?"

"Anything I could." His smile was small. "In case my neat logic turned out wrong and they started shooting."

One man with a club against automatic rifles. It told me something about what had happened down there in his jungle. A good man to have on our side. It told me more about him too.

"Where did you get your military training?

He went on smiling his small smile, his pale eyes still shining and alert, but not really seeing me. A distance on his face, dreamy, and he rolled the steel bar back and forth on my desk with the flat of his hand.

"You know your work, don't you? I was in the Marines. What was your branch?"

"None. Merchant Marine. No fighting, but some swimming."

"The Second War? I missed that one. It seems so long ago now, a different world." He nodded as if he didn't always agree with himself but did this time. "My father was regular army, a sergeant. He told me all about that war. I don't think I understand it, the motives and principles. Seems to me the sides were all mixed up, no clear idea of where everyone's interests really were."

"It seemed clear to us at the time."

"Did it?" He rolled the steel rod. "I grew up in Kansas, went to Stanford, got out in 1960. Phi Beta Kappa and all, but I looked at the executive trainee jobs the companies offered, and joined the Corps." He laughed. At himself, or at the world of corporate trainees, I didn't know. "Good thing I did. I don't think I'd have made it down there in the jungle without what I learned in the Corps. You never know, do you?"

"You usually use your training sometime, somewhere," I said. "Any training, sooner or later."

"You could be right. I made lieutenant at Quantico, bucked my way into the First Force Recon company. That was pretty fair training to help a man get survivors out of a jungle."

It was also the Marine Corp's most elite outfit, with a list of training schools that would make even the toughest shrink: cold weather, escape and evasion, parachute attack, scuba diving, demolition, survival, and worse. You had to be a determined man.

"Where'd the medicine come in? The research?"

"I didn't see much future in the Corps after a few years, so quit and went to med school. Research is where the real frontier lies in medicine, new drugs and methods. Worked for the government for a time after my residency, then saw the new work Kern was doing and got them to take me on. The old man was still there then, and I talked him into sending me down to South America."

He talked easily, without any special emphasis, but I could see his pattern. He set an objective, something he wanted, and he moved straight toward it, quietly but firmly. Phi Beta Kappa at a good college, the Marines, an elite unit, medical school at an age a little older than most, research, South America, and a hospital when every force was against him. And he was handling Bradley Kern's problem the same way. Use anyone and anything that might help Brad, firm and direct.

"Those two gunmen are from South America," I said, "and they know a lot about Bradley Kern. Any connection to your South American experience, Craig?"

"I don't know." He picked up the steel rod again, feeling its weight. "I've been thinking about that myself. Kern has contacts all over down there, and Brad used to ask me about it all quite a lot. Nothing specific, and I'm out of touch these days, but Brad is a boy with ideas. He and Anna Botha are both idealists."

"Those gunmen didn't sound like they thought Bradley was exactly out to do good."

"No, they didn't, did they?"

"They seemed to think Brad and Cebellos had some kind of dangerous caper going. Money and murder."

"It did sound like that."

I waited, but he didn't go on. He was as careful with his judgments and speculations as with his opinions.

"You were coming to see me?" I said.

"To tell you that Wally Kern thinks his desk was searched. Nothing missing, but he tapes all his conferences, and he's sure the tape of our discussion the other day had been played back."

It probably explained how Sam Tower had reached Luz Cebellos. If he'd heard all we knew about Brad and Cebellos, a few simple questions would have turned up that Nestor had a sister. For now, I'd keep that to myself too.

"Someone at the Laboratories?" I asked.

"Probably," he agreed. "What did Marjorie want with you?"

"For me to work on the side for her. To help Brad if I could, and report everything to her. Or so she said."

He thought about it. "But you wonder what she really wants? Some angle?"

"Something," I said. "Bradley might have been up to more than you or Wallace Kern know."

"You mean with Marjorie?"

"With someone. Maybe Marjorie just knows about it."

"Or Cebellos knew about it and was using it."

"Unless Brad and Cebellos were partners. A scheme to rip off Wallace Kern."

"Then Bill Kern is in on the scheme too."

"Not necessarily," I said. "Or it could have been just Bill and Cebellos using Brad's trouble for a squeeze."

Craig stood and paced the office. Silent now except for the hiss and rumble of traffic outside in the rain.

"There could be a great deal we don't know," Craig said, and stopped to look out my window. "Sometimes I think it was easier in the jungle. At least simpler."

"Uncomplicated," I said.

"Yes." He turned to me. "You better find Bill Kern."

◼ ◼ ◼

"Automatic rifles?" Captain Gazzo said.

I listened to the hiss of tires out on the rainy avenue, and to the busy voices in Gazzo's office at the other end of the telephone line. With Craig gone, I was alone in the office. Had I locked my door when Craig left?

"Two of them," I said into the phone. "Asking questions about Cebellos and my client's son. Looking for something."

"They shot Cebellos?"

"Sounded like they would have and could have."

"A Latin war come north?" Gazzo was silent at the other end. "Damn! It fits Cebellos all right. All sides against everyone. He probably crossed them, got eliminated."

"How did he cross them, and about what?" I said. The shadows of my office-home seemed to move, lurk. I was jumpy. "They're still loose and looking, Bill Kern's still missing, and so is the money."

"All right, we'll find your *pistoleros*," Gazzo said. He sounded tired again. "Dan? Don't play hero. Not in my city. I want this quiet and sure. No shoot-outs. You hear me?"

"You won't get any noise from me."

I don't get in the way of automatic rifles. Not with an iron bar, not even with a tank.

* * *

The brass gleamed on the black door. Newly polished. Constance Hall had her priorities. She opened the door.

"Yes?" Her smile was polite, gracious.

"Miss Hall? I'm looking for Bill Kern."

"Bill?" A dark cloud crossed her round face. Literally. The cliché was the only phrase. A palpable darkening that would have been seen from the back row of any theater. She bit her lower lip. A solemn nod. "Come in, Mr.—?"

"Dan Fortune."

I stepped into the single room with its tiny rooftop terrace, still neatly and carefully divided into its separate areas like a miniature townhouse—or the stage set of a townhouse. The overlush crowding of too many hanging plants, too many tall lamps, and the walls of dramatic photographs and packed playbills. She gestured to a chair. I sat down. She sat facing me, her legs crossed smoothly—Lesson Five in any theater class.

"You're a friend of William's?"

"Private investigator. I'm looking—"

Her smile was sad, "For his wife?"

"His brother."

"Brother? What does his brother care about us?"

It was her first genuine reaction, and the gracious lady diction slipped. Simple middle-class midwest, and something else. A faint slurring. She'd been at one of the bottles her sweet neighbor had mentioned. And the gracious voice and manner wasn't her only act. Short, she wore high heels long out of style, and a loose black dress intended to look elegant—and to hide a shapeless figure and a flabby belly. Close, her round face was puffed, dull, and grainy like a swollen orange. At about forty-five she looked every hard year.

"His brother cares about eight thousand dollars of his money that's disappeared with Bill."

"Money? His brother is accusing—!"

"His brother knows him, and so do you. Bill's gone, and the money's gone. He was here last Monday. Where is he now?"

"I don't know!"

"Does he come here often? Not just on a spree?"

"He comes to me when he can." The gracious lady slid back over her like a silent curtain. A tragic lady. "We love each other, Mr. Fortune. It isn't easy for Bill, I try to help him all I can. I don't expect you to appreciate that."

Her voice was sad again, gentle. Star-crossed lovers. She looked at her walls of photographs and playbills, gestured toward them.

"I have my work. Twenty-five years. Times have changed, my kind of work is out of fashion. The commercial theater is all skin, violence and mumbling. I accept that, work where I can. Off-Broadway, community theater. I've had offers to go to smaller cities where real theater is still alive, but I do hate to live far from Broadway." She sighed. "But William is a lost soul. A prisoner of a world he can't live in and can't escape. We try, but—"

"There's a midtown hotel with a regular game," I said. "A hotel where he takes a room sometimes."

She shook her head. "I won't help his family to hound him, badger him."

"Not his family. He could be in danger." I told her about the two gunmen. "They could be looking for him too."

"Guns?" she said. "Murder?"

"Do you know the name of the hotel?"

She was still looking at her walls of photographs. I had the feeling that she sat in that chair looking at those walls a great deal. Her past.

"The Saint Charles, perhaps," she said.

He was the only one sweating.

Six other men sat around the green table in the third-floor room of the St. Charles. It wasn't hot. A hand ended as I came in. I couldn't see his face, but it seemed to follow his cards as he threw them in the way a blind man follows the sensation of light.

In the smoke of the hotel room on the ragged edge of midtown, bottles stood on a bureau with the Gideon Bible. Only two players had glasses at the table. Five were in shirtsleeves, tieless. Arizona Dutch Stahl wore his suit, vest and tie, as erect as the chips stacked in front of him.

Bill Kern also wore his suit coat, but his tie was loose and his collar twisted and wet. He sat with his back to me, tall, silent, and more rigid than erect. He didn't move when I came in. Unaware of anything but the cards.

Dutch Stahl did move. He looked at me, at Kern, at his watch. He shook his head. I understood: I wouldn't have long to wait, there was no point in breaking into the game.

I sat down in a corner and waited.

The cards went around twice more. The two players with glasses drank. Another made jokes. There was a large bet. Dutch Stahl raised the bet. Bill Kern called. Dutch won. The next dealer shuffled, dealt a new hand. He didn't deal Bill Kern in.

Shoulders square, Bill Kern sat there as the cards went around, as the two drinkers drank, as the joker told his jokes for the new hand. Someone won the hand. Bill Kern buttoned his shirt, straightened his tie. He nodded right and left, stood up, and turned from the table. The game continued behind him as if he no longer existed, had never existed.

He walked to the door. A stiff-legged walk. The way a man walks who has been sick and doesn't trust his legs yet. He went out the door. I went after him.

"Kern?"

In the empty corridor he stopped. I saw him stiffen. He turned slowly, almost forcing himself to turn and face his fate. Tall and lean, unsmiling, the eyes set deep in his long face dull and resigned. The eyes blinked at me, brightened. He didn't know me. Perhaps there was some mistake.

"Your brother sent me to find you," I said. No mistake.

The brightness left his eyes. His thin mouth was as stiff as his walk.

"Then that's it, isn't it?"

"Anything you need to get from your room?"

"Yes, there is."

We walked along the corridor.

"You were hard to find," I said. "A special reason?"

"You found me."

We took the elevator up one floor.

"It isn't necessary to come with me. I'll meet you—"

"I'll come along," I said.

His room was at the far end of the main corridor.

"Any of the money left?"

"No."

He unlocked the door, switched on the light, and I followed him into the room.

The lights went out. Hands held me. An arm squeezed my throat, choking. . . .

■ ■ ■

There was light. A small, plain, dim room with one lamp.

Bill Kern sat in an armchair facing me. His eyes were open and looking at me. That same pain and confusion I had seen in his eyes in the photograph. Looking at me, but not seeing me.

"Who was it?" I said.

It was an effort. My throat hurt as if something were stuck in it. I tested my lone arm. My face. My body. I was all there in another chair facing Kern.

"I told them," Bill Kern said.

"Told what?" I said. "Told who?"

"They attacked you in the dark. I didn't know what was happening. I'm not much good at physical action, never was. The thinking type. A euphemism for a weak man. Like Hamlet, I lack gall." He almost laughed, but didn't. "When the lights came on you were unconscious. I couldn't fight them. Everything about Cebellos, about Bradley, about what Wally . . . "

Stiff in the chair, he let his voice trail away.

"What about Cebellos?" I said. "Is there something you know I don't? More than helping Bradley Kern in Mexico?"

"More?" He blinked at me. "I don't know."

"You went to give Cebellos the money Friday night?"

"I gave Cebellos the money. On Friday night."

"You *gave* him the money?"

"Eight thousand dollars. I don't know what happened after that. To the money or to Cebellos."

His voice had gone toneless, like a parrot. He had already said he'd lost the money. Talking in circles, incoherent. I began to wonder if they, whoever *they* were, had worked on him, too. Maybe drugged him. Or was he telling me something?

"Did you kill him, Kern? Grab the money?"

"Of course," he said. "They'd ask that right away."

I watched him, and it wasn't drugs. It was just that his mind was on a lot at the same time. In more than one place. In space and time. Here with me, back there reliving last Friday night, and wandering across the city in between.

"You planned to say that you gave Cebellos the money," I said. "So that you could keep it, gamble with it."

"He was dead." Kern took a deep breath, slowly. "I got there late, after midnight, and he was dead. I had the money, you see? Earlier, I mean. In my hands. I had some drinks. Eight thousand dollars. I had quite a few drinks. But Wally had trusted me. It was for Bradley. I had to meet Cebellos."

His dull eyes were large in the dim light. "He was dead. On the floor. I ran. I ran away from that room. I had to call Wally, tell him."

"But you didn't. You called your wife."

"I was afraid. Who had killed Cebellos? Why? What did it mean? I . . ." He shook his head again, as if hearing himself and not even believing himself.

"You had eight thousand dollars. You had to gamble."

He was silent. When he spoke again, he was calmer.

"Cebellos was dead. I could have given him the money. I would have if I'd been on time. Who would know if I said I'd given it to him, he was killed later, and the money was stolen? Eight thousand dollars. No one could know. Weak idiot!"

So back there last Friday night he talked himself into believing that he could say he had given the money to Cebellos, and everyone would think that the killer had taken the money. Later, he realized he'd never get away with it. Where had he gotten the money to gamble? Either he had never given it to Cebellos, or . . . ?

"When did you realize the story wouldn't work?"

"Saturday. Sunday. I don't know."

"Why not go home then? Tell your brother the truth?"

"I'd lost. I had to win it all back, didn't I? I always have to win it back, make everything right again."

He was the kind of man who sneered at his weakness, but went on being weak. It was a good enough story, it fitted him, and only a dead man knew for sure if it was true or not.

"Who attacked me, Kern?"

"I don't know who they were. Two of them. They had guns, spoke Spanish. A heavy one with a mustache, and a young—"

"What did you tell them? Exactly!"

"Everything. What else?" Despising himself again. "All Nestor's scheme to free Bradley. The money Wally paid him. What he'd done so far. How he and Adelita were going down there again with more money to bribe—"

"Adelita? She was in it, too? You told those gunmen that Adelita was working with Cebellos?"

"Yes. Cebellos said a woman could do things a man—"

"Get your stuff. Now!"

He got a raincoat and a paper bag. I pushed him ahead of me out the door and down to the elevator. On the floor below the room where the game had been was empty. Smoke still hung in the air. I called Captain Gazzo.

⠿ ⠿ ⠿

Gazzo got to the Marquis Arms first.

A small crowd had gathered in the rain, and the wet iron lions shone red in the revolving light of the patrol cars. In the narrow lobby the desk clerk was calming startled residents.

On the seventh floor the door of 7-H stood open. I left Bill Kern with the patrolman guarding the door, and went in. Two of Gazzo's detectives turned to look at me. The captain didn't. He'd gotten there fast, but not fast enough.

"Minutes," Gazzo said. "Still a pulse when we got here. God damn!"

Adelita Stahl sat in a straight chair at a table. Adelita Stahl who had been Adelita Cebellos, twice, and who had wanted to be Adelita Cebellos a third time. If she made it, it was going to have to be in some other world. She'd wanted to be with Nestor Cebellos, and she was. She was dead.

"How?" I said to Gazzo.

He nodded to two glasses on the table. I smelled them. One had cyanide in it. Gazzo went on staring at the dead girl as if he'd never seen a corpse. He'd seen a thousand corpses. It wasn't that. It was the young, the eager, the innocent.

"Anyone see those two gunmen?" I said.

"We're asking. We're looking." Gazzo glared at the dead girl, an impotent rage in his eyes. "A patrol car got here two minutes after you called. There was still a pulse ten minutes ago! How did they get out? Not downstairs."

"Maybe they were never here," I said. "Poison?"

"Guerillas. *Pistoleros.* Never taken alive, right? That's the stupid code, right, Dan? The pill. The capsule."

Gazzo went on just standing there. We all did. As if waiting for something. Maybe an explanation. The explanation all of us, somewhere among the shadows inside us, want to hear when death strikes down the young, the full-of-life. We didn't get that explanation, no one ever does, but a change came over the room. An arrival, large and filling the room. I turned.

"Addie?"

Arizona Dutch Stahl stood tall and dignified in the open doorway, flanked by a pair of patrolmen. After the single word, his daughter's name, he stood there for a moment, silent. Then he strode straight across the room through us all to the dead girl. He looked down at her, his long hands folded in front.

"We broke up early. The game. The Texan had to buy us all a drink. Big loser. Some things you have to do."

The tall old man stood there over his dead daughter. Then he reached out and touched her. He touched her shoulder, and then her face. His hand moving over her face as if to comfort, to soothe away her pain and her sadness.

"Who?" he said. "What happ—?"

The shots came from a distance. Two shots, and then a burst of rifle fire. Somewhere above us.

"The roof."

Gazzo was first into the corridor, toward the fire stairs. I was last up the dark stairwell. I had no gun.

Inside the roof exit a patrolman breathed hard.

"They shot at us! Sergeant's out there!"

The police went out. I listened to them pound across the hotel roof, spread right and left toward the adjacent roofs.

"Police! Throw down your guns!"

I slid out low into the rain and darkness. A rifle fired from ahead toward the street parapet. I heard a low grunt.

I crawled. Two detectives kneeled over a fallen shape. On his back, he lay with his eyes wide open in final surprise. Captain Gazzo. One of the detectives stood up in the rain.

"They killed the captain! Get them! God damn it, go and get them!"

I sat with Gazzo. Close to him.

Four more policemen were hit. One seriously.

The two gunmen were shot to pieces. The gray-haired *pistolero* with the bandit mustache, and the young one with the hot eyes.

They would run through no more nights.

12

I delivered Bill Kern. Wallace Kern paid me. I didn't know what he planned to do about his brother, or his son, and I didn't care. I didn't care about Arizona Dutch Stahl, either. I suppose he buried Adelita, but I didn't know when. I wasn't invited to the funeral.

Every life is made up of pieces of a thousand other lives. We are part of everyone we have known, loved, hated, worked with, fought, helped or harmed. I don't know who said that first, probably some caveman, and it's as true as most ideas, and probably as false, and I'd known Captain Gazzo a long time.

I wasn't invited to his funeral either, but I went.

They gave Gazzo the usual inspector's funeral, and more. For this one they all turned out, from the Mayor down to Gazzo's female sergeant in the blue skirt that had never ceased to puzzle the captain. The Commissioner was there, the Chief, Chief of Detectives McGuire, and every off-duty detective in Manhattan.

His wife wasn't there, or his children. He'd never had either. His filing cabinet was his family. The criminals and victims he'd spent his life with. They weren't there, or maybe some were, hidden and silent. There was only the work. His life and his death. The Mouth, Preacher Gazzo, gone to join the long row of shadows he spent his life with on the hazy edge between light and dark.

I was there, if no one spoke to me, and I listened to them bury Captain Gazzo, and then I took a long walk through our city.

We'd never had time to be friends. No one seems to have time for friends today. Too busy, and in a sense our work is all any of us are or can be. But it isn't work that keeps us too busy, it's success, and that is something else. Success isn't enough. He could have been my father, at least my stepfather, and somehow you don't talk about the past with a man who knew your mother better than you did.

I had a few Irish whiskies. I walked some more. Uptown, and downtown. I had some more Irish whiskies.

Where was I going to get the benefit of the doubt when things went bad? I would work in a different world.

I walked east and west.

The gray November river.

* * *

The knocking on my door was restrained. Firm, but polite.

A thin November sunlight at my windows. Almost a week since Gazzo and the gunmen had died, and it had stopped raining. Had it rained at the funeral? I couldn't be sure.

I got out of bed and opened the door.

"You were in bed?" Arizona Dutch Stahl said. "I'm sorry. I'll come back later."

He wore a hat, a tie, and a velvet-collared gray herringbone over-coat. A Chesterfield. I hadn't seen one in years. A warm coat. It must have turned colder out in the city.

"Take some coffee instead," I said.

"Thank you."

He came in carefully, tentative, not sure of what to do with his hands. Hands that actually wore gray suede gloves. Always formal, a little stiff, he moved now something like a robot. A black armband on the sleeve of the Chesterfield.

"Take a chair at the table," I said. "I just have to plug the coffee in, wake up a little."

By the time I'd washed and dressed my always-ready coffee had perked. Stahl sat at the table where I'd put him, stiffly erect, his hands folded in the gray gloves. His face was stone, except for a faint, bright stare to the eyes as if seeing what had been, and might have been, and never would be. Going over the past day by day, and the future year by empty year.

"Sugar?"

"Black."

I poured the coffee, sat down.

"I buried her," he said. "Addie. On Monday."

He took off his glove before he picked up the cup. I'm not one who mourns the loss of genteel manners. Mainly they separated the few with the time to learn them, from the many with no time for anything but work. But they were Dutch Stahl, his style, and that's the whole secret—to live your own style.

"My sister came. First time in fifteen years. We're a strange country, the different moralities of a hundred years all at the same time. To bury the dead, she speaks to me."

Like Wallace Kern that first day, he was talking too much. A taciturn man. The tip of his pain.

"I'm a gambler. All I ask is to end each day with enough to play tomorrow, and if at the end I've broken even I've won. But everyone has days when he wonders if whatever he's doing is good enough. Maybe she was the only real product I had."

"Something doesn't sit right, Dutch?"

He sipped his coffee. "Those gunmen killed them. That's what the police say. She was working with Cebellos, and those two gunmen killed them both."

"I know they were looking for anyone who'd been working with Cebellos, Dutch. That's true."

"Yeh," he said. "I knew Cebellos pretty well. He had no ethics at all, and a lot of enemies. With his dirty deals and slimy life, he had it coming. Those gunmen were the kind to get him in the end, and Addie was working with him." He looked up at me. "But I don't like the feel of the deck. It feels short, not all there."

"What's missing?"

"I knew him, and he knew himself. Gunmen like those two, he had to know they were after him. He was shot up close with a handgun without a fight."

"They caught him short."

"He wasn't even armed. No gun in his apartment."

I said nothing.

"They had automatic rifles. A handgun killed Cebellos, poison killed Addie. They had the heavy weapons for the cops."

"Go on."

"Addie hadn't been near him for a year, or near Mexico. She was having her third operation, to be pretty. She was ready to go back to him, but she didn't. He found her. He came to her with a job. A job,' Fortune, not a plan."

"How do you know that?"

"She told me." He drank his coffee, drained the cup this time. "He could always con her, use her. He came to her and told her he'd been 'hired' to do a job in Mexico. Not a scheme of his own, a real job, legitimate. That's what she said—a legitimate job, and he was going to take her back, and they'd go to Mexico, and everything would be smooth. Enough money to go straight in Mexico. Honest money, not some rip-off."

I poured him more coffee. "So?"

"Cebellos never had a legitimate job in his life. Maybe he meant it when he said he could go straight after the job, but no job he got could have been legitimate. He had nothing to sell that wasn't crooked. I want to know who hired him to do exactly what?" He took out a bill. It was a five hundred.

"Have you told all this to the police?"

"Yes. They were polite."

The police are overworked, they need more than a father's doubts. I took the five hundred. Stahl stood up.

He pulled on his glove. "I've been a hustler all my life. It cost me my wife, and that was all right. Addie was something else. Most fathers have a home. I had hotel rooms, and Addie. Maybe those gun-men killed her, but I want to know."

◼ ◼ ◼

Cold. A thin sun with snow somewhere behind it pushing the crowds faster along the streets, and even the iron lions at the Marquis Arms were grayer and lonelier at their guard.

I asked the desk clerk about visitors Adelita might have had, strangers hanging around the lobby in the days before she died, any-one he had noticed the night she died. I told him I was working for Dutch Stahl.

"You'll have to speak to the manager." He picked up his desk phone. "Mr. Karkian? There's a Mr. Fortune out here asking about Miss Stahl. Yes. He's been employed by her father. Yes. Very well." He hung up. "He'll see you as soon as he finishes with a guest."

I sat and studied the lobby. Even if there was a rear entrance, there was no way to reach the elevator or the stairs without being seen from the desk, and the clerk would never have missed the two gunmen. But Gazzo would have said if the clerk had seen them. Then how had they gotten up to 7-H? Over the roofs? That sounded like guerillas.

It was half an hour before the clerk sent me down a side corridor to the door at the end marked: Manager.

"Come in."

The man who stood against the closed door didn't look like a hotel manager. Neither did the one who pushed me into a chair, and I didn't know either of them.

I knew the man behind the desk. He wasn't a hotel manager.

"Dutch Stahl now?" Chief of Detectives McGuire said. "You change clients fast, Fortune."

"He wants to know who killed his daughter."

"He told us," McGuire said.

"It looks like you listened."

The one who had pushed me into the chair said, "Say we don't like a private opening a closed case on his own." He was in a chair tilted against a wall. Dark blond, trim and compact in a well-pressed blue suit. "Especially a cop killing."

"No." I shook my head. "You had the hotel staked out. Your man had me stalled until the chief could get here. You listened to Stahl's doubts, and you heard them."

"We didn't have to listen to Stahl," Chief McGuire said. "We'd come up with the same questions ourselves, and a few more. We found other guns where those two Latins had been holed up, but Ballistics can't match the bullets in Cebellos to any of them. The girl was poisoned in a drink. Would she really have sat down drinking with enemies of Cebellos? His killers?"

"They could have duped her, Chief, or forced her," the one in the blue suit said. "They could have ditched the gun they used to kill Cebellos."

"They could have, Pearce," Chief McGuire said. "This is Captain Pearce, Fortune. Acting in Gazzo's command."

Pearce couldn't have been much over thirty-five and already a captain. A bright young man, and I got older every day. It was going to be a very different world to work in. But not quite yet. Chief McGuire was still running this show.

"But it wasn't the kind of gun I'd figure those gunmen to have," McGuire said, "and from Fortune's report of his meetings with them, they didn't sound trigger-happy. More talk than killing, and a lot of questions."

"Perhaps they got their answers," Pearce said.

"Not much time for questions," I said. "They couldn't have had much more than half an hour after Bill Kern told them about Adelita to locate her, get to the hotel, ask questions, and kill her. They probably knew about her, and knew where she lived, but that still doesn't give much time for questions. They moved hard and fast, and they were guerillas not assassins. I'd have expected them to use their rifles, not poison."

"Amateur psychology," Captain Pearce said. "I can do it too. In a hotel, shots could have caused a riot. Bad for them."

"All right," Chief McGuire said. "They probably killed the girl and Cebellos, but we want to be sure, too. For Gazzo." He leaned back in the manager's chair. "They were Bolivian rebels, and the Bolivian generals have congratulated us. It's praise we can live without. There's a lot of flack about racism and fascism from our Third World friends. We can handle that right now because they were shot resisting arrest for two killings. But what if they hadn't killed anyone?"

"Nasty," I said.

"Worse. If they didn't kill them, we want to know who did, because that would be who really killed Gazzo. But we don't want to open up a hornet's nest. You see the problem?"

"You want the truth, but you don't want anyone to think you don't already have it. Not until you're sure."

McGuire nodded. "We can dig into Cebellos and those gunmen, that's okay. We can even check quietly on Adelita Stahl. But that client of yours, and his son, are in Connecticut and Mexico, and we don't want other police involved until we know more."

"You want me to dig into Wallace Kern?"

"We couldn't be involved openly."

The police have work to do any way they can. They wanted to use me. Did I have a choice? Yes, I could say no and walk away. Sure I could. And find work in another country.

"Dutch Stahl thinks Cebellos was hired to do what he was doing," I said. "Not the moving force."

McGuire stood up. "Find out. Pearce has everything we got from the desk clerk. He'll fill you in, be your contact."

McGuire took the silent man at the door out with him. That left me with Captain Pearce. I had to get used to it sooner or later. Pearce teetered in his chair, eyes half closed.

"Luz Cebellos visited Adelita at least once on the day of the shooting. The clerk saw Adelita with a big man in some kind of field jacket and boots—six-feet-two, two-hundred-and-twenty, dark-haired. The clerk thinks the big man was around the lobby at other times. Mean anything to you?"

He was quick, precise, efficient. A new era.

"No." But I thought about the unseen man who had put the knife to my back and asked questions in the park.

"There was a nervous man in a cheap leisure suit who sat in the lobby and made the clerk suspicious, and a tall, skinny guy in a hat and overcoat. Old-fashioned the clerk said, very proper and prim. He came in perhaps twice."

"The first I don't know. The second sounds like a man named Sam Tower." I told him about Sam Tower's snooping.

"Then he's your target." Pearce smiled, briefly.

"You really think those gunmen didn't kill them?"

"I don't know, but we'll work on the assumption they didn't. We'll assume someone else did, work from there."

Most of the time the police have to work on some assumption. It's a place to start, and there's nothing wrong with it, as long as they don't try to bring it into court instead of evidence.

"Do a job, Fortune, and we'll get along," Pearce said. "Gazzo thought a lot of you, I hear."

"We knew each other a long time," I said.

"I hope we'll do the same, but I'm not Gazzo, and I run a tight ship. I like facts, not inspiration."

"College?"

"Yes, majored in criminology and law."

"Times change," I said.

"The new breed." He smiled all the way. "You're going to love me."

13

The taxi took me along the Connecticut country road. Since I had come this way first all the leaves had fallen, and the big houses were clear through bare branches in a cold sunlight that moved toward December and the first snow. The visible faces of victory that had bothered my father so much. The identity and power he had ached for, but had never known how to have, and in the end could only hide from.

The big houses. A car for each day. The real mark of success since our history began—to have a great deal more than you, or anyone, needed. Someday the mark of success will be to have *almost* as much as you need. It will be better, but a lot will be lost, and I don't think there'll be a place for a man like me. A new world with a different dawn and different birds singing a different song.

◼ ◼ ◼

Sam Tower wasn't in his office across the corridor, and I saw no one else I knew at Kern Laboratories. Wallace Kern was polite but stiff. A busy man, bulky at his desk, impatient.

"Was there something wrong in your payment, Fortune?"

"I just want to talk."

"Talk?" His solemn eyes were sunk in his fleshy face. "But it's all over. Finished."

"You don't sound too happy about it."

"My son is still in a Mexican hellhole."

"He might have been anyway," I said. "It's possible that Cebellos was jobbing you. Playing two sides for himself."

"I don't care." His boyish face was stubborn, dogged. "I don't care what Cebellos was doing, with us or anyone else. He was at least a hope. Now we have no hope. Where do we start?"

"If it was some rip-off, Cebellos probably wouldn't have done much to help your son."

"He *did* help him!"

"The move to another prison, and some privileges?"

"Perhaps it was little for the money, but it was something, and Cebellos had a plan—" Something crossed his soft face, dark like a pain. "You don't think it's over? Someone else going on with Cebellos's plan? You think—?"

"If anyone was, they'd contact you. For money at least."

"But . . . ? Then why do you think it's not closed?"

"I have a client who has doubts."

"Client? You don't mean that Marjorie has—!"

"Jacob Stahl. Adelita Cebellos's father."

"The girl those guerillas killed?" He blinked at me, swiveled. "Then you're not concerned with us anymore?"

"I'm not sure what I'm concerned with," I said. "Did you ever consider that Brad might be guilty? Mixed up with Cebellos in something down there? Then used Cebellos to get money from—"

"Guilty?" He stared at me. "How does that come into it? He's my son! Guilty or innocent he belongs in America with his own people. Guilty of what? Some mistake? Some Mexican crime?"

"Most Mexican crimes are American crimes too," I said. "My client suggests that Cebellos wasn't acting on his own. That it wasn't Cebellos's idea to contact you through Bill, offer to help Brad. Someone hired him to do it."

"Hired him? Why? Who?"

"Any possibility it could have something to do with your company, your business? You make drugs, right?"

"Not in that sense, no! We deal in medicines, not dope!"

"Medicines can be drugs, and people deal in them. A lot of supposedly legitimate companies have dumped extra drugs on the illegal market, and drugs are scarce in Latin America."

"Kern Labs does not 'dump,' legally or illegally! And we have no operations in Mexico at this time!"

"Someone in the company? Unknown to you? A little private plan to make some extra bonanza?"

"If you're thinking for an instant of Bradley, don't! He would never do such a thing, and he couldn't!" Kern was angry, breathed hard. "We have strict inventory control, and every ounce of our production is accounted for."

"Some extra production? If not Brad, someone else?"

"Impossible. We're not a large company. I would know at once if anything were irregular. *Anything!*"

"You thought your wife might have hired me. Why?"

"Tom Craig told me she'd already tried, and she's been away from home, running around. I don't know where or why."

"You think she's worried about Brad?"

"Probably. She is his mother."

"Could there be some other reason?"

He got up from his chair, big and boyish, and walked to one of his windows that overlooked the whole plant. He looked out only briefly, as if reassuring himself that it was all still there, and then began to circle the office studying the walls.

"Marjorie is a restless woman, horrified of growing old. She refuses to be a matron, or even a housewife. That's not unusual now, many women are striking out on their own. But Marjorie always refused to be a housewife, and we've been married over twenty years, yet never had any idea of striking out on her own. She likes the advantages of being a well-off wife."

His voice was more sorrowful than bitter, and he went on circling the office. His eyes were down now, like an overweight adolescent after a date that hadn't been what he had hoped.

"From the start she had to have excitement. Life had to be fun, full of big occasions. If there wasn't some event, she'd create one. She would make every night a bacchanal if I let her. I have work, and I keep her from it, but I pay a price. She only wants love as part of an event. When I refuse to party half the night, it separates us."

I hadn't asked about his sex life or his marriage. So he was telling me something else—that he didn't know what Marjorie was doing, but that she was a woman who had to have events, action, and who might create her own.

"You know a short man who wears expensive suits but sleeps in them?" I described the rest of the man who had met Sam Tower in the Plaza washroom. I didn't mention Tower.

"That must be Fred Sarguis. He's president of Caldwell Pharmaceuticals, one of our competitors," Kern said.

"Does Bradley know him?"

"We all do here. Why?"

"Any special trouble with him? Recently?"

"He's a sharp rival in business, but that's all."

I got up to leave. "Got your brother locked in a dungeon?"

"Bill? He's back home."

"No punishment? For the eight thousand?"

"The money is gone, he can't get it back. Thanks to you, he didn't have time to lose anymore."

"He will," I said.

* * *

The blue car bumped hard into the rear of the taxi.

"Hey! You stupid—!" The taxi driver opened his door.

"Stay put," I said. "No damage."

In front of Bill Kern's house Anna Botha's short black hair blew in the November wind. Her blue eyes were large. I paid off the taxi driver.

"Shit," he said, drove away.

"Who were they, Dan?" Anna Botha said. "Those two gunmen?"

"Bolivian guerillas."

Her hair blew—and tall ostrich plumes. They were in her wide eyes, the savage plumes of a violent history.

"He'll never come back," she said. "Bradley. They'll kill him. Whoever they are, whatever it is."

Laura Kern stood in her doorway under the low eaves.

"Who is it? Anna?"

"And Dan Fortune," I said.

"Mr. Fortune? Well come in, both of you."

Anna Botha was wearing a loose gray skirt that swung around her fine legs as she walked ahead of me. A blue shirt, and she huddled in a mismatched red ski jacket in Laura Kern's shabby living room. The low-ceilinged room was scrubbed and polished, as if Laura Kern had spent all morning cleaning. Bill Kern didn't appear. Laura sat on the couch, motioned us to seats.

"Thank you for returning Bill, Mr. Fortune."

"How is he?" I sat down.

"Bill? He's—"

Anna Botha didn't sit down. "They've all forgotten him! Bradley. No! They haven't forgotten. They don't want him to come home. Someone!"

"What makes you think that?" I asked.

"No, Anna," Laura Kern said. "I'm sure that's not so."

"Yes!" Anna said, fierce. "Look at it. That Cebellos was helping him. Wallace paid money to free him. Cebellos is dead. The woman helping him is dead. The money is gone. The gunmen who killed Cebellos are dead. They had to know what is going on, and so they're dead too!"

"The police killed them, Anna. If anything, they were Brad's enemies, the other side."

"How do you know for sure what 'side' they were," Anna said, "and perhaps someone wanted the police to kill them!"

Was it a guess? Speculation? Groping for anything.

"You have anyone in mind, Anna? Who set them up?"

She sat down now, hunched over. "No."

"I don't understand," Laura Kern said, looking from one of us to the other. "What sides? What is happening to Bradley?"

I said, "Anna is sure that Brad didn't go to Mexico just for a vacation."

"Those gunmen prove it," Anna said, almost toneless. Her mood had changed. Subdued, the savage fire gone. "Marjorie said they tried to kill her, talked about Bradley. Questions about anyone involved with Cebellos and Bradley. About who sent Cebellos and Bradley to Mexico. Who hired Cebellos."

"Did someone hire Cebellos? Send Brad down there?"

"That's why I came here," Anna said, looked up at Laura. "Bill knew Cebellos before he brought him to Wallace. He has to know more than he's said. He's probably part of it."

"He wouldn't hurt Bradley, Anna," Laura Kern said.

"I want him to tell me," Anna said. "He'd sell his soul for gambling money."

"He's not here just now," Laura said. "I'm sorry."

Her voice was light and casual. A quiet smile, as if Bill were out on some trivial errand. But I sensed strain underneath. I didn't think Bill was just out buying a pack of cigarettes, and she hadn't mentioned work. Anna Botha stood up.

"Then I'm wasting time," she said, but she didn't move to the door. Motionless, as if not sure where she had to go. "Bradley and I often quarreled with his father over the obligations of a business company. Its duty isn't just to make money, but to help people. Especially a drug company. No one is isolated, not even a business. That's what brought us together, made us so close. The idea that life is working to help everyone everywhere. Now—?" She turned to the door, looked back. "Now I think perhaps its going to be what ends us."

"Anna—" Laura said.

But the girl was gone. Outside the blue car drove away in the rising November wind. There was a storm somewhere. Laura looked at the closed door for some time.

"She thinks Bradley went to Mexico on some kind of mission? A plan?" Laura said, turning to face me.

"Yes," I said. "Laura, where is Bill?"

"He stepped out for a time. Just—"

"Laura?" I said. "The truth. Why isn't he at work?"

She was silent again, studied her hands. "He lost his job. I don't know where he is. He . . . " She looked up at me. "He was different this time, Dan. When he came home. After one of his runs he always comes home contrite, ashamed, worn out. He sleeps for days. This time he wasn't contrite, more bitter than ashamed, restless and keyed up. As if—"

"As if the binge wasn't over? Does he have money?"

"I don't know," she said. "He was changed, Dan, almost nasty to me. Indifferent to me, to his guilt. Nervous. I felt still alone, he didn't need me this time. I cleaned all morning today to keep busy, hoping he'd call, but he hasn't called."

"He was gone all last night again?"

"Yes." She shivered on the couch, her eyes helpless. "I felt a gulf between us. Not the same anymore."

I got up. "Did he say he was working for anyone?"

"No," she said. "Dan? Find him again. Please."

14

The November storm still threatened in the dark blowing sky over the city, but not in Jamaica. In the surly streets heavy and airless with sullen faces wandering aimless under an invisible dome, weather has no meaning.

I rang at Luz Cebellos's side of 2670 New York Boulevard. There was no answer from behind the patched and blanket-covered windows. The door was open. I went up to the second floor warily. There was no sound inside the bedroom where I had talked with Luz and the two gunmen. I opened the door.

There was no sound, but the room wasn't empty. The Latin dandy with the pencil mustache, glistening hair, and massive biceps lay on the bed. On it not in it, fully dressed and alone. Smoking. Not a cigar this time.

"Luz?" I said.

He smiled. At the blank wall. He smoked deep and slow. The sharp, acrid, pleasant odor of marijuana filled the room.

"Hey, *amigo*. She don' work here."

"Where does she work?"

He took out a comb. Slowly. Held it in both hands as if bringing it to him from a distance. Carefully combed his hair.

"Where does she work?" I said.

He nodded. Combed. Picked up the stick of pot again.

"I love her, yeh? I mean, yeh. No way, you know? Work a junk truck. What you gonna do?"

"Where do I find her, *amigo?*"

He smoked. Deep. Slow. Throat quivering.

"The city. No bread in Jamaica. In the big city, Forty-eighth and Seventh. Look around. The Taft. You find her."

"Thanks."

"*De nada.*"

■　■　■

High in the rolling clouds the tall glass building disappeared like some menacing giant with a thousand eyes and no head.

Caldwell Pharmaceutical Company had its offices on the twenty-third floor. Behind double glass doors and a vast maroon carpet a steel-blue housemother commanded the reception desk.

"Do you have an appointment with Mr. Sarguis?"

"Tell him Mr. Sam Tower sent me."

She performed her duty crisply, looked at me curiously as she replaced the receiver. "Mr. Sarguis will see you. Left along the corridor."

I had a hunch Mr. Sarguis had not told her to send me back quite that politely. An under-secretary met me, and held me in abeyance until number-one secretary came to usher me through her sanctum to heavy double doors and into an echoing corner office behind them.

"Sam Tower never sent you, mister."

At an endless desk he wore what looked like the same rich brown suit stained with the evidence of more than one meal. A brown bag lunch was spread around him in the glittering office with its wide view of the clouds.

"He didn't send me, but he's what brought me."

"Who are you?"

"You know who I am. Tower told you in The Plaza washroom."

"The private eye?" He leaned back in the chair that was twice his size. "So what do you want?"

"What do *you* want?"

He smiled, pudgy hands clasped behind his head.

"You and Sam Tower," I said. "What do you want with your competitor's top employee? What are you waiting a while for?"

"You work a lot in washrooms, Fortune?"

"As long as people do business in washrooms."

"Sam Tower and me, we are friends, okay? Many years. Old Kern, he would have understood that. Old competitors, old friends, eh? Comfortable. Sam wants to talk, I listen. He isn't so sure the son would understand."

"Talk about what?"

"Personal matters. Not your business."

"Just talk? No schemes? Deals?"

"Sam Tower doesn't make shady deals."

"Is there some shady deal? At Kern Labs, maybe?"

"I hope so." Sarguis grinned. "At least some trouble. I have more of the market than Kern, but I'd like all of the market, right? That's called good business."

"Is Sam Tower going to help you get all the market?"

He leaned across the desk toward me. "You are fishing, Fortune. Insinuating. I don't like that. I don't ask cute questions, and I don't answer them, okay? What I do in my business, is not your business, okay? Play somewhere else."

The door opened behind me. Number-one secretary stood waiting in the doorway. Sarguis had pushed some button.

I left.

* * *

I had a steak and a bottle of Cabernet at Downey's. It was dark when I came out, and the wind blew me hard up to Forty-eighth and Seventh Avenue. It was early on the crowded avenue, the women working quiet and discreetly. In shop doorways, casual against the walls, they blended with the crowds, unobtrusive until some passing man looked at them with a hair more than a passing glance.

The Taft was two blocks north on the east side of the avenue. By the time I got there I'd seen a lot of smiles from the shadows. Only smiles now. It was too early for more vigorous offerings, too many tourists and families on the streets who had to be protected. Until midnight, or so, the police would be stern. After that they would ease off, turn to more serious work, and the action here would get more blunt.

Luz Cebellos wasn't behind any of the shadowy smiles.

She wasn't around the Taft.

I stopped at a smile on Fiftieth Street. A tall, bony blonde with a fierce smile and breasts so large for her rib cage they seemed to have been borrowed from another woman.

"The best, honey?"

"I'm looking for Luz Cebellos," I said.

"She's not worth the price."

"Neither am I." I held out a twenty. "Know her?"

"Cop?"

"No. Private problem."

"She likes the classy theater act over toward Broadway." She took the twenty. "Thanks."

It took over an hour, and then Luz Cebellos found me.

"I thought it sounded like you," she said.

"Word moves fast here."

"It's a tight club," she said. "Sometimes."

The hordes of night people pushed all around us on the glittering Broadway sidewalk, the traffic crawling horn to bumper. Only the tourists looked at us, curious.

"Working or playing?" she said.

"Working."

"Then you can buy me a drink."

The café was two steps down from Forty-eighth Street, small and quiet, with a narrow bar inside the entrance, tables at the rear, and dim booths near the bar. We took a booth. She ordered tequila. I had beer. The waiter eyed me, poker-faced.

"Regular work?" I asked.

"When I'm strapped. A good dollar, fast and easy."

She drank, sucked lemon. She wore a sleek black dress that made her look thinner. Her thick black hair tied back on her neck, panty-hose and high heels, a simple silver chain that touched the swell of her breasts. Not a peasant, and less Indian. Cool and exotic.

"Not so easy," I said. "Not such a good dollar."

"You know?" Salt, drink, lemon. "You don't know. You're not the type that buys, and you don't have the tools to be a seller. I don't like or dislike, for or against. Just the way it is. Something I can use in any corner."

"At a risk."

"Everything's a risk, sooner or later. Not too bad when you work alone. Off the street mostly, some good regulars."

She signaled. The waiter brought us two more. He knew her. That put me in a category. I didn't protest. It would only make him nervous to know I wasn't the usual customer.

"Did those *pistoleros* kill Nestor and Adelita?" I said.

"The police say so," she said. "I don't know. Probably."

"How did they get to you?"

"Through Nestor, I suppose. From Mexico perhaps." She enjoyed the salty tequila, the sharp lemon. Tasted it for a time. "They came out to Jamaica, walked in on us cold. My friend out there isn't much good in that kind of action. They wanted to know all about what Nestor had been up to, who else was with him, who hired him. You heard them."

"Who did hire him?"

"I'm not sure anyone did. It looked like one of his games. Maybe someone else with him, and using Adelita as usual."

"Bill Kern, maybe? The someone else in with him?"

"I don't know a Bill Kern."

"You knew Adelita, went to see her the day she was killed. For those gunmen, or for yourself?"

She was a bright woman, she knew what I was doing. She tasted salt, drank. I was putting her with Adelita the day the girl died. On her own with a murdered girl involved with her murdered brother, or a finger for two killers? Lemon.

"They didn't know about Adelita when I was with them. Not as far as I could tell. I don't know how they found out. I went to see her to try to find out if perhaps she had killed Nestor herself. Your suggestion, remember?"

"What did you find out?"

"Adelita couldn't kill anyone. Not even Nestor." Her tequila glass was empty. She looked at her watch, shook her head to the waiter. "I don't think she could have killed even *for* Nestor, and I knew that before I went to her. I really went after the money, I suppose. You made it clear there was eight thousand good dollars floating around somewhere, and I thought that Addie could have it. Or she could know who had it. There was even a chance I could inherit the whole action, whatever it was. Those rebels were after something that had them very worked up. It could have been worth while."

"But Adelita didn't want to play ball?"

"She wouldn't admit there was anything to play. She insisted Nestor had been doing some legitimate job, getting a clean stake to set up an honest career in Mexico. A fresh start for the two of them. Nestor!"

Her voice was scornful, but it was the same thing Adelita had told Dutch Stahl. Obviously it was what Nestor Cebellos had told Adelita. Only was it true? Or partly true. Or just another of Cebellos's crooked stories to con Adelita?

"The desk clerk at the Marquis Arms saw three other people around the lobby and Adelita." I described the nervous man in the leisure suit, the big man in boots, and Sam Tower. "They mean anything to you? Did you see anyone else suspicious?"

"That tall older man sounds like the one who knocked on my door before you did."

"What did he want?"

"I never spoke to him. The rebels chased him off when I said I didn't know him." She turned the empty shot glass in her dark hands. "I don't know that one in the leisure suit either, but the big man—?"

"He means something to you?"

She raised the glass, got a drop or two from it. "I saw a man with Nestor. Perhaps twice, a month or so ago. He looked like some kind of outdoor type, hiker, ex-soldier. Not Nestor's kind at all. Hard and rootless-looking, you know the type. No home, a drifter, professional troublemaker."

"Who did Nestor say he was?"

"He didn't. I didn't ask. His business."

Questioning is a matter of context. The guilty will lie, and answers must be judged. Her last answer sounded like Nestor, I believed it. The other answers I couldn't be sure about. She looked at her watch again.

"When I went to see Adelita that day," she said, pulling her coat on, "a woman was coming out of her room. Tall, dark blonde hair, shoulders like a man. Addie called her Laura, said she was a friend of a friend."

"Laura?"

She stood up, buttoned her coat.

"How much will you make the rest of the night?" I said. "We could talk."

She laughed.

15

East Sharon, Founded 1707, Pop. 6031.

Cold and motionless, like the black methane seas of Pluto, the Sound lay dark through the trees behind the house in the moonless night with the storm gone and the wind down.

An old Victorian house behind a low wrought-iron fence and small lawn in a row of Victorian houses on the side street of the old Connecticut town. A neat village, the houses close to each other but not too close. Town, not country, but with room to breathe.

The small letter box read: Sam'l Tower. I found a place to park my rented car. It wasn't easy.

Seven cars almost filled the wide street under three dim street lamps, and the noise came from Sam Tower's house. Through the high, bright, narrow windows I saw ladies in a Victorian living room set with small tables and straight chairs. Ladies bustling with trays, talking low in pairs, at the tables opening new decks of cards.

There were no men.

I rang. The doors were dark, carved oak. Double doors, and tall, with iron fittings from a hundred years ago. The girl who answered was in her late teens or early twenties.

"Mr. Sam Tower?" I said.

"I'm sorry, he's—"

"It's important."

"You can talk to mother, I guess."

The long entrance hall was the same dark oak as the doors, with sliding doors on either side, an open door at the rear to the pantry and a busy kitchen, and stairs going up. The sliding doors on my right were closed. On the left they were open showing the large living room full of women and heavy old furniture. The girl went through the room to where a short, stout woman presided over a coffee urn on a buffet table piled with refreshments. The image of the girl, in her early sixties, she wore a motherly flowered print and came out to meet me.

"Can I help you, Mr.—?"

"Dan Fortune. I'm looking for Sam Tower. Your daughter didn't say where he was."

"She's a good girl, our last at home. They grow up so fast, don't they, Mr. Fortune?"

"Usually," I said. "If Tower isn't here, I—"

"My husband's at home, but he's quite strict about never being disturbed during a board meeting. Perhaps, later, you—"

"It's important, Mrs. Tower. What board? Kern Labs?"

"Heavens, no. Samuel isn't a member of the Kern board." I sensed a quick chill in her voice, but it passed, turned into a kind of pride. "Our Board of Selectmen. Samuel is First Selectman, has been for I don't know how many years. In the town, they respect him. He usually holds an executive meeting before our bridge game. Efficient, he says, with all the selectmen here. How important is your business?"

"It's about the trouble at Kern Labs."

She blinked at me. "You're the detective Wallace hired."

"Yes I am."

"I'll tell Samuel."

She left me in the hall, went back toward the rear. I heard the voices now in the room behind the closed sliding doors. Men's voices. She must have gone to another entrance into the room. She came out through the sliding doors.

"Go in, please, Mr. Fortune."

She didn't go back to her post at the coffee urn, but stood just outside the double doors as I went in. Eight men in suits and ties, none young, turned to look at me. They were seated in an informal semicircle on chairs and couches in what was a very English and old-fashioned library-study. A semicircle around a Georgian marble fireplace with a small fire in it.

Sam Tower stood alone in front of the fireplace, his back to the fire, the focus of the semicircle and the meeting. He gave me a short nod, obviously not pleased to be interrupted in his importance.

"Something urgent, Fortune?"

"Same thing, new questions," I said. "Can we go somewhere?"

"These are my friends."

"Suit yourself," I said. In the warm, solid room all the men watched me. Behind me I sensed the women. "You went to see Adelita Stahl, or Cebellos, at the Marquis Arms. Why?"

"I've told you that. More than once."

"Protecting the company?"

"As best I can."

"From what? You've never told me that."

"From mistakes. From duplicity. Wallace has made more than a few unwise decisions, and I sense that he's making another. Something is happening. Wallace can be gullible."

A heavyset man turned on the couch. "You listen to Sam, mister. He knows Kern Labs like he knows this town."

Another said, "The Board over there, the stockholders, they don't know what goes on. I got stock myself, that young Kern never has talked to me. If it wasn't for Sam there, I'd sell and fast."

Like a chorus, they all took it up.

"Someone got to look out for that company, protect Wallace Kern from himself and that crazy son of his."

"Sam and old man Kern started together."

"When the old man died, Sam should have taken over."

"Better than young Wallace or that useless Bill."

"Sam should have been made president."

"We all know that."

They were more than Sam Tower's friends and fellow selectmen. In East Sharon, Tower was large, and I saw them all more clearly. Older men, rural, the suits not fitting too well. Suits bought from the racks of local shops, the ties and shirts ten years behind the fashions of New York shops. Local men, not the newcomers from the city who slept here and worked there. These were men who worked in East Sharon, with weathered faces and roughened hands. The businessmen, boatmen, craftsmen and shopkeepers. And Sam Tower was one of them—the successful one who had risen high beyond the town in a big company. The first citizen of East Sharon.

"Everyone expected Sam would be president."

Tower smiled. "I said they were my friends."

"Fred Sarguis says he's your friend," I said. "Does he expect you to be president of Kern?"

Tower didn't smile. "Rachel, why not start setting the tables, and serve the coffee. I'll join you shortly."

The stout wife's voice rose bright and busy, herding them all into the bridge room, fussing over their refreshment needs. Sam Tower remained at the fire. I stood where I was as they passed around me, faded away, and the heavy doors slid shut. Tower rocked on his heels, hands behind his back, the Yankee captain on his quarterdeck.

"You went to Sarguis? Why?"

"To talk about you."

"I don't like that, Fortune."

"Neither did he," I said. "Nothing to hide, though. Just old competitors, old friends. You wanted to talk. Maybe about some shady deal at Kern Labs. Not your deal, or his deal, of course, but he pops up, and you dig through your boss's desk."

He teetered for a moment, then crossed to a smoking stand and filled a blackened pipe. He puffed until it was going well, and then sat down. I stood.

"Cebellos," I said, "Luz Cebellos, Adelita Stahl. You've been moving around. Why Adelita? Because you knew she was working with Cebellos? Do you know who else might have been?"

"When Cebellos was killed, it was clear to me that he had been up to something devious and obviously dangerous. Something that involved the company, or Wallace, or both. I did not know what. The police brought the Stahl woman out of the apartment where you had found Cebellos. I had to find out if she could tell me what Cebellos had been doing."

"Could she?"

"Only that Cebellos had some job both here and in Mexico."

"You knew her only because the police brought her out of Cebellos's apartment?"

He smoked in clouds. "Wallace did not see fit to take me into his confidence, preferred to rely only on Dr. Craig, but it was no secret to me that something was wrong even before Wallace hired you. Since Bradley went to Mexico and got arrested. What was he doing down there? He's a damned fool, but he's no drug addict."

"Not a vacation? You agree with Anna Botha?"

Tower snorted. "That one! Her work may be adequate, but she's a dangerous radical, arrogant, and a mulatto at that. It would be no surprise to me if she was behind the whole thing, the way she leads Bradley by the nose, twists his mind." He had the pipe in his teeth. "And Bill Kern. He was distracted, nervous, even before he went on his binge this time. I'd have thrown him out bag and baggage years ago, but not Wallace. He even had him working for him."

He looked at me over the pipe. "You asked if I only knew the Stahl woman because I saw the police bring her out. Well, I didn't know her, but I knew the name: Stahl. After Bill Kern's last fling over a year ago I had to settle some of his bad checks. More than one of them was to a man named Jacob Stahl. I remembered the name, and that's when I realized how deeply that Cebellos had to be involved with Kern Labs."

Pipe smoke almost hid his eyes. "And that's when I went to Fred Sarguis. As he said, we're old friends, old competitors. There's not much that goes on in the pharmaceutical business he doesn't know. I wanted to know if he had heard of any unusual sales, any unexplained large purchases of drugs."

"Had he?"

"No, nothing. And just to be sure, I did some night work on our production and inventory records."

"All accounted for?"

He nodded. "But all this is too much to be about a boy in jail for smoking some marijuana. There's more, Fortune, and I intend to go on trying to find out what."

"For the company," I said.

"Yes," he said, began to knock out his pipe. "For the company."

⬛ ⬛ ⬛

I drove toward New Canaan. To look for Bill Kern. Yes. To ask Laura Kern why she had gone to Adelita. Why she hadn't told me about it. How did she know Adelita?

A car is much better for trips to Connecticut. More convenient. Absolutely, Danny boy. This time it was much better to rent a car. To talk to Tower, look for Bill Kern who probably wasn't in Connecticut.

No timetables, no waiting taxi drivers. Come and go when you pleased. Or stay.

She was alone, unhappy. Bill had been different this time. She felt alone.

⬛ ⬛ ⬛

The small house showed light behind the white fence. I parked, got out, stood in the dark night looking at the lighted window under the low eaves.

In what room?

The living room. I was sure. A woman alone. I rang.

"Dan?"

Her hair was loose in the doorway, dark blond around her angular face and shadowed eyes. On her broad shoulders.

"Is he home?"

"No."

She stepped back. I went in past her. The light was in the living room, and the television was on. She watched me from the archway into the room.

"You forgot to mention that you went to see Adelita Stahl at her hotel. The day she died. I didn't know you knew her."

She sat down on the couch. I took an armchair. The light of the droning TV flickered between us.

16

"When Bill called me the second time to say he was all right, had a room at a hotel, I knew that he was different. He sounded odd, tense, almost distant. Detached from me, from everything, as if he wasn't going to come back this time. I was afraid. I couldn't just wait anymore."

"How did you know Adelita?"

She was wearing a faded housedress, took a pack of cigarettes from the pocket. She lit the cigarette.

"Wally had told me about Nestor Cebellos and the money by then. That he'd sent Bill with the money. That it had been a mistake. That Cebellos was dead, and Bill and the money were still missing. That had frightened me, and after Bill called and sounded so strange, I had to do something."

The housedress was loose and open. Her skin was smooth, flowing down from her throat and rising to the hidden breasts.

"I didn't lie to you, Dan. I don't know where he goes or who he meets when he gambles. But he talks after he comes home. Randomly. Unconnected stories, names, places. Nothing definite. But once he talked about a girl. A young girl, little more than a child. The daughter of a gambler named Arizona Dutch Stahl. He seemed to know Stahl well, spoke of him at other times. The girl was a sad little thing he wanted to help. A girl who never smiled, thought she was ugly, and was mistreated by a Mexican husband she had married not once but twice."

The loose hair brushed her mannish shoulders. Under the dress I saw the outline of her hips curving from a long waist.

"I remembered the girl and her name. When I called Wally and Tom Craig to tell them I'd heard from Bill, I asked them if an Adelita Stahl had any connection to Nestor Cebellos. They told me she had, and where I could find her. I went the next day. I had to try to help Bill if I could."

"How much?"

"I don't understand what—"

"How much would you help Bill? If he killed Cebellos after all, and Adelita knew that, how much would .you do to help him?"

"He didn't kill Cebellos." Positive. No possibility of doubt. "The girl knew only that Cebellos had a job, and that somehow it was Bill who had gotten it for him. As a favor."

"What else do you know that you haven't told me?"

I was angry. The dress moved softly against her thighs.

"Nothing, Dan. I only talked to the girl. All she knew about Bill was that he gambled with her father, and was nice to her. She seemed to be in a kind of trance, a daze."

Her fingers long on the cigarette.

"Connie Hall? A woman he sees in town?"

"Yes, I know that." She looked away. "Not her name, I never asked. He only sees her when he gambles, runs."

"You're so sure?"

"I'm sure." She put out the cigarette. "I suppose we all need someone. To share when we win, to comfort when we lose. He's ashamed to include me. I want to be with him, would go with him, but I understand his need to keep me from it. He doesn't want me to see him then. So he goes to her. I'm at home, the safe harbor when the frenzy fades and he wakes up alone in some hotel room. Then he comes home to me."

An understanding in her voice and her eyes. Gentle. Even a triumph. He came home to her.

"But not this time? Not the same?"

She flinched like a startled deer in headlights. From the couch she stared at the television set where a young man in carefully too-tight pants writhed with a microphone. She got up, turned off the set, and stood looking down at it.

"His father never had time for his children. An old father, already successful when he married, and his real child was the company. Not an original story, but it's always original for the child, isn't it?" She searched herself for a cigarette. Her pack was on a table. I gave her one of mine. She looked away.

"Bill was the first boy, the one who would carry on. What time his father gave him was for the company. Production, profit, sales. Bill was a poor student, and he grew to hate business. He had no feel for it, no skill, no interest. A terrible disappointment to his father." She shrugged. "The mother was a narrow, religious woman who didn't really like men or boys. As Bill grew older she gave all her attention to Wally, the 'baby.' But she knew what was proper, and when Bill resisted his father she called him a wild ruffian, a juvenile delinquent sure to end badly. Rejected by both parents, or so it seemed to him, and I suppose always will."

She looked down at the empty TV screen as if it would come to life and show her something important. It didn't, and she looked up at me. She smiled. A resigned smile for the way life happened, involved in her story of Bill Kern. Not her eyes. Her eyes, as they looked at me, seemed to belong to someone else, to be in some other place at some other time.

"So he gambles," I said. Her eyes were large, hollow. "He gambles and runs so that someone will chase him, pay attention to him. He can't hold a job, so people say he'll end badly."

"When he was young he painted. He was good, he won prizes, but he wasn't good enough, and he couldn't do commercial art or illustrate. He couldn't paint or draw on order, or he wouldn't. When I met him he was trying to become an anthropologist. He was no good in classes, in academic research. Too restless, but he loved the field work, the far places, the strange people, the freedom. Then he had to give that up."

"Why?"

"He married me, had to take jobs to support a wife." She smiled again. "He would have found some other reason to give it up, of course. Some way to fail. There's no answer to his restless need. The world simply doesn't have what he needs in it. Except me, and waiting for time to run out."

No sense of anger, no hint of any urge to revenge for what he did to her. Only the gentle understanding of his needs.

"What about your needs?" I said.

"Mine? Yes, I have needs."

She glanced around the small room. Right and left. She looked at an ashtray, put out the cigarette. She sat down on the floor in front of me, her legs under her Indian fashion, the loose skirt a prim tent revealing only her feet.

"You brought him home. He came home, but not to me. Not this time." She slowly rubbed her legs through the dress. "I never felt it like this. He was different, isolated. He had nothing to say, no guilt. He was still somewhere else. Something had happened out there, not just his fling or his weakness, not just the other woman. He didn't need me, Dan."

I said, "I do."

"No, you don't need me."

"All right. I want you."

She nodded, looked down at the floor. She sat there on the floor with her head bent and the dark blond hair hanging like a waterfall over her thin face. I raised her head with my lone hand.

The women I meet are in trouble, alone, lost for the moment, and they come to me for that moment. Not this time. This time it wasn't like that. This time I wanted it to be for more than the lonely moment of trouble and loss.

I hadn't wanted that in a long time.

◼ ◼ ◼

In the ringing of the doorbell she moved beside me. Heavy and near. In a half dream.

"Dan?"

I lay there in the dark bed. There was no sound beyond the doorbell. New Canaan. My watch read one A.M. She lay close against me, long and warm.

"Bill?" I said.

She didn't move away from me. Body to body.

"He wouldn't ring."

Quiet. Calm. Maybe it was this time. I got up.

"I'll look."

Across the narrow bedroom the front window looked out to the street and the front door. The figure at the door was vague, shapeless. A woman's hair. The car at the curb was a small red Mercedes. Marjorie Kern.

"Your sister-in-law," I said. "Let her in?"

"No. Come back to bed."

She had one of those lean bodies. The breasts solid on the rib cage, the belly almost flat as she lay on her back, the small high mound curving down. Her large hands were light on me.

"*Laura! Bill! Are you in there?*"

Who shouted on a New Canaan street at one A.M.?

"She's stubborn," I said.

"But impatient. She bores easily. She'll go."

Rhythmic hands searching me, soft and playful. The doorbell was furious at being denied.

"What does she want this late?"

"I don't know, Dan. Anything. Important or trivial, she'd act the same. She does what she thinks of when she thinks of it. If it's anything at all, she'll come back."

"*Laura!*"

I said, "She's been disappearing, busy doing something. Wallace says he doesn't know what or why. She tried to hire me to work for her as well as Wallace."

"To report to her?"

"For Bradley. I wonder what she really wanted me to report to her, what she wanted to know? What she's doing."

"Some man, probably." She laughed. A light laugh. "Listen to me."

The bell violent and angry. *"Laura! It's Marjorie!"*

"There's a difference," I said.

"Is there? What?"

"With you it happens, happened. An experience, not a triumph. A moment, not an ambition."

"You make it sound clean."

Rapid footsteps walked away from the door. Annoyed.

"I hope it is," I said.

"How do you know how it is for Marjorie, Dan?"

"People tend to do everything the same way. I'd take a guess that she's never been with someone she really wanted, only with someone she's collected."

The car started, squealed away. The street silent again.

"Poor Marjorie," Laura said. "Perhaps it's not a man this time. Perhaps she's just very worried. For Bradley."

"She's worried, but I'm not so sure about what. It might be better if it is only some man."

"Then I hope it is. A good man. Happy. For her, too."

Her hands found me again, and I turned to look down at her in the dark bed. Her arms rose around my neck, pulled me down to her as she opened to me.

17

Again toward dawn.

And for me, now, beyond the beginning or the ending of a job. Bill Kern a different man. When I found him again he would be someone else. A separate world of three.

"Laura?"

"You'll bring him home," she said. "Go to sleep."

In the echo of a dream the sunlight came bright and cold from sleep with the rapid click of heels long past dawn. Too long past dawn. The doorbell bringing back my job.

"*Bill! Laura!*"

Laura got up, put on a robe. "I'll let her in. You'll want to talk too, stay in bed."

For her too? A commitment?

"Well!"

Marjorie Kern stood in the bedroom doorway. White and mink. An all white pantsuit, dark hair pulled back and tied in morning haste, her hands thrust into the mink. Smiling.

"You can be had, Mr. Fortune." She turned to Laura who sat on the bed. "You're finally showing some sense, Laura. Give the men back their own. Bill deserves it."

"I don't have to get back at men, Marjorie. Not Bill or anyone else."

"You're doing it though, aren't you?"

"What do you want, Marjorie?"

"I want Bill. Where is he?"

"I don't know."

I said, "What do you want with him?"

"You're sure?" Marjorie chewed her lip. "I've got to talk to him."

"I'm sure," Laura said. "He hasn't been home for two nights. I don't know where he is, or what he's doing. It can't be any gambling, he has no money I know of."

Marjorie bit a fingernail. "Yes he does. I gave him money. A thousand dollars."

"What for?" I said.

"You don't give Bill money, Marjorie!" Laura cried. "You knew that. Now it's gone."

"What was it for?"

Marjorie turned on me. "You wouldn't let me hire you! You wouldn't help me. Not me! I had to know what is going on! What Wallace is doing to free Bradley, if anything! I won't be shut out, treated like some child or incompetent. I know they're all in some action together. I paid Bill so he would report what they do, but he hasn't contacted me. Not a word!"

"And he won't." Laura shook her head. "Not now. Not until the money is all gone."

I said, "They? Who are *they*, and what action do you mean? Cebellos's scheme to free Bradley?"

"Wallace and Tom Craig. Bill. Bradley. Perhaps Anna Botha, too. And it's more than Cebellos bribing Mexicans. It was going on before Bradley went to Mexico. I know that now."

"Tom Craig and Bradley?" I tried to see behind her anger. "Before he went to Mexico? What was going on?"

"I don't know for sure, something. Bradley was acting like some juvenile conspirator, skulking around at night." She bit another fingernail. "A thousand dollars. That stupid weakling! I'm a fool, you're right. Ridiculous failure. How can you stand him, Laura? How could you go on living with such a zero? Even working at a job for him. He'll never be anything but a total failure."

"A man is more than success," Laura said. "Every person is a lot more than success or failure."

"A failure is nothing. What good can a man who fails be to you?"

"You don't love a man just because he can make life easy and secure for you, Marjorie. You don't give love for that."

"For what *I* give, Wallace had better be a success."

"Isn't he already?" I said.

"Daddy's company," she said. "I'd like a man to be a bit more than that. On his own."

"It gives you a thousand dollars to throw around," I said.

"I'll throw another thousand, even two, if you'll do what I want. Report everything you learn to me—first. And find Bill."

"I'll find Bill, but not for you, Marjorie. On the other, no."

"An honest man?" Scornful. "I'm sorry for you, Laura. You don't choose men very well, do you?"

"I suppose not."

Marjorie Kern turned and walked out. Her heels clicked in rapid anger on the walk. The Mercedes drove away. I held my hand out to Laura. She took it, but moved no closer on the bed this time. She squeezed my hand.

"He has money," she said.

"Maybe from more than one source."

She nodded. "He'll always take money, from anyone. He'll say he can do whatever anyone wants whether he can or not, tell them what they want to hear."

"That can be dangerous."

"I'm afraid for him, Dan."

I heard a difference in her voice, subtle, but there. She had talked of being afraid before, frightened, but then she had been afraid for herself, for the two of them. Now there was a detachment, objective, afraid for him. Or did I just want to hear that? A change in her life.

"When he's pushed, restless, on the gambling," she said, "he doesn't act rational."

"I'll find him, Laura."

She squeezed my hand again.

* * *

Promises are easy. If Bill Kern were gambling, finding him again would be easy enough, too. Not quick, but sure. If he was up to something else, it wouldn't be that easy, and finding Bill Kern wasn't what the New York police had asked me to do.

I didn't care what the New York police had asked me to do. I wanted Bill Kern. I drove out of New Canaan toward the Merritt Parkway and New York.

I noticed the red car when I left New Canaan. It came out of a side street a block from Laura's house and drove behind me. For a time it was two cars back. It was still there when I reached the parkway. A small car. I didn't have to see the radiator to know it was a Mercedes.

Marjorie Kern was tailing me.

In a red Mercedes! And too close. I almost laughed aloud. I didn't laugh, though. I had a client, orders from the NYPD, and it was too important a chance to miss. Bill Kern would have to wait. I passed the Merritt Parkway and drove on south with the Mercedes still two cars behind me.

I drove on past the Turnpike toward the Sound. I wanted a road to some marina or small boat dock. I found one. A narrow blacktop off the main road that turned to an inlet and then turned again long and straight toward the Sound. The inlet was on the left and small streets of big houses on the right. I waited at the last turn until I was sure she had seen me. (The Mercedes nosed around the far turn behind me, and stopped with a jerk. It takes training.)

Around the corner I jammed down the accelerator. One eye on the rearview mirror, one on the first side street ahead. I reached the street before the Mercedes appeared, swung into it, backed into the first driveway, and watched.

The Mercedes passed the side street and went straight on toward the water.

I drove back to the corner, and watched until the Mercedes disappeared down the long back road in the distance. Then I drove back the way we had both come to the main road, went across it, and parked half a block beyond between a van and a Cadillac. If I was right, the only way back to the main road for anyone who didn't know the area was the way we had gone, my rented car was an ordinary dark blue Chevy Nova, and she would never have gotten my license.

I was right, at least about the route. Some twenty minutes later the Mercedes appeared driving angrily. I grinned into the rearview mirror, and then stopped grinning. Instead of coming back past me the way we had come, she turned right on the main cross highway!

I made a fast U-turn, but had to wait before I could turn into the east-west highway. Luckily, a red Mercedes is as easy a car to tail as there is. She was a quarter of a mile ahead still going east. Not for home or Kern Laboratories.

I settled as far back as possible, even losing sight momentarily rather than risk being noticed. She went straight on, making no stops or turns, and I was sure she had no idea she was being followed. As self-centered as she was, she probably hadn't even realized that I'd spotted her tailing me, thought she lost me by plain bad luck.

East Sharon, Founded 1707, Pop. 6031.

I came alert, but when she left the highway it wasn't into Sam Tower's street. A long road leading to the East Sharon Yacht Club. I dropped back out of sight, and drove on slowly. The road ended at the yacht club, with a marina, a tavern, and vast parking lots. I parked at the far rear of the lot nearest the road out, and walked among the cars toward the docks and boats. The red Mercedes was parked in front of the tavern.

Marjorie Kern was still in it.

Out of sight among the parked cars, I watched her. She sat there. She smoked. A half an hour passed. An hour. She did nothing, and I realized what she was doing. A stake-out. I was watching her. Who was she watching? Or waiting for? I found out.

The old car parked near the boat docks. Bill Kern got out on the driver's side. Luz Cebellos got out the other side.

Marjorie Kern got out of the Mercedes.

Bill Kern and Luz walked out on the docks. Marjorie went after them. I brought up the rear. Kern and Luz reached a big cabin cruiser with a high flying bridge and swordfishing outriggers, climbed aboard, and went below. Marjorie Kern stopped. She stood on the dock looking at her watch. After five minutes, she followed them aboard the boat and down below.

I moved carefully. No one was on the deck of the cruiser. I slipped aboard, crawled to a porthole of the main cabin, and looked down into it.

Marjorie was talking angrily. Luz Cebellos and Bill Kern sat on a cushioned locker. Marjorie wasn't talking to them. Her anger was directed at the other man in the plush cabin—Dr. Tom Craig.

Craig wore a dark Navy pea jacket, heavy denim jeans, and a black turtleneck sweater. He said nothing as Marjorie raged. Luz Cebellos said something. Marjorie turned on her. She snarled at Luz. Luz sneered. Tom Craig spoke—short and sharp. Marjorie sat down, looked up at Craig. He. . .

"Get up slow."

The point of the knife in my back. Again. The same voice from the park a week and a half ago. The same knife. I got up.

"Walk forward." The same steady, unhurried voice.

I walked forward. A hatch was open near the bow. The knife prodded me.

"Go down."

I went down a steep, narrow ladder. The hatch closed above me, locked, and his heavy footsteps went away aft.

In the dark I struck a match.

I was in a small room with oars, rope, spare parts and the odor of gasoline. There was a low door. It was locked.

I sat down on a coil of rope.

Nothing happened for some time. Only voices talking somewhere aft, arguing.

Then the voices stopped, and the engine started. The boat was moving. I felt the gentle swell of harbor waters, and then the growing surge of the open sea.

18

Cresting the waves, the boat seemed to be making good speed when the small door opened.

"Come on, Fortune."

His green army-style pants were bloused over low paratrooper-style boots. A faded khaki field jacket full of pockets, a green turtleneck sweater, and a red beret. At least six feet two, two-hundred-and-twenty pounds. Dark hair a shade too long.

"You're one up on me," I said.

"Joe Ryan."

He turned and walked bent down along the low companionway. Legs slightly apart, he walked balanced to the roll of the boat. Behind him I bounced from wall to wall as the boat rolled and pitched. I didn't see the knife on him. It could have been anywhere, from the boots to the pockets of the field jacket.

We emerged into the main cabin. There were six bunks, a long table, a bar, some armchairs, and a small galley.

"Wait here." The big man, Ryan, went up on deck.

Luz Cebellos still sat on a cushioned locker. Marjorie Kern sat in an armchair, holding on. Bill Kern wasn't there now, but Wallace Kern was. He stood over his wife. No one spoke. Tom Craig came down. He leaned against the long table.

"I'm sorry we had to handle it this way, Dan," Craig said, "but after those gunmen we're not taking chances. It seems some people want to stop us, if we don't know why."

"Stop you from doing what?"

"Wallace?" Craig said.

"No, you go ahead, Tom," Wallace Kern said.

Craig sat down, his legs stretched out in his spray-wet jeans. "We didn't lie to you, Dan. Bradley's problem is as we told you, Cebellos was doing what we said he was, and we don't know why those gunmen killed him and the girl."

"But?"

"When Wallace could get no help legally, he asked me what to do. I told him the truth—in a Latin country only one way was left—direct action. Brad would have to escape, and it was up to us to arrange it."

"So Dutch Stahl was right? It wasn't Cebellos's idea?"

Craig nodded. "I knew Bill had met some shady people in his gambling. I told him we needed a Mexican national willing to make a good dollar who didn't much care how. He got us Cebellos, and Cebellos brought Ryan in. They went to work to arrange the escape. Brad was moved closer to the border, and we were allowed to contact him. Cebellos, Ryan, the girl Adelita, and I were about to go down and finish the details when Cebellos was killed, Bill ran with the money, and we hired you to find him so that we wouldn't be mixed up in a murder."

"That's how you could tell Laura where Adelita lived," I said. "Adelita was working with you."

"With Cebellos. Not our idea," Craig said. "And I wish we knew why those guerillas were after them."

"Bolivian rebels. From your part of the world."

"Don't you think I've thought about that?" Craig brooded. "Is there some connection? I haven't had any contact with down there since I was forced out, but it can't be a coincidence. Did Bradley use my name? Is there more to his arrest than we know? Something hidden?"

"Something that makes the Mexicans want to keep him," I said. "That made them hold him out of the prisoner exchange."

"Whatever," Craig said, "I don't like it. They were my people down there. I liked them, I'd fight for them. But even if Bradley hurt them somehow, we're going to get him out of that jail. Bring him home without the damned prisoner exchange."

"No matter why he's in the jail?"

Wallace Kern said, "He's there for no reason. None."

"We have it all arranged," Craig said. "Miss Cebellos has agreed to take Nestor's place with the Mexican contacts, but I'd like another man. There's Bill, only we can't even trust him to run errands after the money incident, and after those gunmen I need someone not part of us up until now. Perhaps you?"

The boat was burying its nose deeper into the waves, heaving high, and rolling more. Marjorie Kern was hanging on, but Luz Cebellos seemed to be enjoying the ride. Wallace Kern was oblivious to the motion, a good sailor and watching me. Their story sounded more honest this time, but it still told me no more about the deaths of Cebellos and Adelita, not to mention Captain Gazzo, and the answer could be down there in Mexico.

"I'll have to talk to my client."

"Of course, Dan. You—"

A hatch slid open above us, Ryan peered down from the wheelhouse. "Squall coming up fast."

"We better head in," Craig said. He started up topside, looked back at me. "Join me on the bridge, Dan?"

Black clouds were piled up to starboard and ahead. The wind teared my eyes as we climbed up to the flying bridge, and squall-gusts heeled the boat over as it plunged into the waves. On the open, wind-swept bridge, Craig took the wheel, grinned.

"Hang on!"

He waited for the waves, spun the wheel, and turned us, wallowing, before another wave could take the boat broadside. Marjorie Kern had come up, and sat in the rear cockpit, pale and green and hanging on. She glared up at Craig at the wheel. Wallace Kern stood near her, braced in the cockpit, his boyish face red in the wind and spray, but calmly watching the turn. Ryan climbed down below into the cabin, and Luz Cebellos had gone far forward to stand near the bow holding the railing, her dark hair blowing and her eyes bright.

"Okay, we're going in," Craig said above the wind.

The turn made, he ran the boat fast before the wind, and I sensed a kind of violent tension. I soon saw why. The marina was inside a natural harbor, and the rocky entrance was narrow and seething with cross current and high, conflicting waves. I knew enough about boating to recognize a nasty passage.

Craig's eyes were riveted ahead on the narrow passage, his face intense, mouth open, eyes glistening. In the bow, Luz had her teeth bared, staring ahead. Through the open hatch I could see Ryan down in the cabin, lying on a bunk, smoking with his eyes closed, indifferent. Wallace Kern still stood in the cockpit, his heavy face unchanged, impassive as we plunged toward the entrance. Marjorie Kern half climbed, half crawled up to us on the flying bridge. Her face was white and angry.

"You can't go through there in a squall!" she cried. "Go out and wait until it calms down! Tom, you take it—!"

Craig laughed. "Enjoy it, woman! You know, Dan, there are only three things still as violent and savage as when the world began: the primitive places, the sea, and man himself. It's primeval and clean, the sea. Here we go!"

"Tom! No! I—"

But it was too late, Craig took the boat straight in, and the rocks closed about us in the narrow, surging passage. The spume of the spray as the cross waves hit the rocks drenched us. Marjorie grabbed Craig's arm. He shook her off as the boat slewed and yawned, sucked backward by the waves, and in danger of losing headway. Marjorie clung to Craig, her arms around his chest, her body pressed against him, her head buried into his back. If we lost power here we were in real danger, and I took a good look around for the best chance if I had to swim.

But even as I looked, not too optimistic about the chances of a one-armed man in the waves and swirling current of the narrow inlet, I thought about something else. About Marjorie Kern. I watched her. Them. Marjorie and Tom Craig.

Then we were through, and running ahead in calm waters toward the marina and the berths. Craig grinned at Marjorie.

"See? No problem. You ruin it by being scared. By being too scared. A little fear, that's normal, adds spice, but too much and you miss the whole game. Come on, we're safe."

She stepped away from him, her wide eyes dark and furious.

"You bastard!" she said, her full lips open and wet.

Slowing the boat glided in toward its mooring. And I watched Marjorie Kern, and knew why she had wanted to hire me. Tom Craig. It wasn't what her son was doing that she wanted to know, it was what Tom Craig was doing.

We docked, Ryan emerging from the cabin yawning and tying the boat up as Craig berthed it. The big man would drive Luz Cebellos home. The others had their own cars.

"We leave tonight," Craig said to me, "if you want to join."

I drove out of the yacht club parking lot. Marjorie Kern and Craig. An affair? She wanted to find some hold on him? He wouldn't be a tame lover, and she was a woman who would want the upper hand. The power, the one who said yes or no, and if just being female wasn't enough she might try for another weapon.

Or was it some other problem?

※　※　※

Dutch Stahl sat in the St. Charles Hotel game as impeccable as always. A light gray suit, it was daytime, with a pale blue shirt, darker blue tie, and a white carnation in his buttonhole. Even in mourning, with a black band on his sleeve, a man kept his style. And if he had style he suffered inside.

"A hundred on the kings," a sweating mark said.

"My bet," Dutch said softly.

The mark hesitated, muttered, looked hard at the three high hearts in front of Dutch and the $6oo-plus in the pot, touched his cards, then abruptly threw in his last $100, crying:

"Three kings!"

Dutch sighed, turned up his ace-high heart flush, and took the money with those long, quick, elegant fingers. The mark stood up, looked at the other players as if about to ask for credit or a loan, then walked out.

He passed Bill Kern coming from the bathroom.

As rigid and unsmiling as the first time I had found him, Kern passed me without recognition. A little less rigid, the erect walk a shade less stiff-legged, the lines of his long face more relaxed. As he sat down in his seat at the table, I saw the chips stacked there. He was winning. Almost a smile at the corners of his mouth.

He hadn't seen me, or didn't remember me.

Dutch Stahl had and did. As I stood behind Bill Kern, someone dealt jacks-or-better draw. Kern held a pair of nines. He saw a $50 bet from a wiry little man who drew three cards. He called a $100 raise from Dutch who drew two. He drew three himself, picked up a pair of Jacks, and raised the opener.

"It's all in what you know," Kern said, smiled.

The opener folded, outdrawn. I waited for Dutch Stahl to jump all over Bill Kern, raise him right off the table. It was a poor hand to raise into a two-card draw. Dutch folded, and stood up. He was looking at me not the game. Distracted? His suffering not quite all inside?

"It might be my night," Bill Kern said.

He raked in the pot with both hands. The hands shook, and his eyes had a savage shine to them. Eyes that saw only the winnings, oblivious to everyone and everything else.

"Nice pot," I said. "How long did you know Nestor Cebellos?"

His hands stopped for a second, and he looked up at me over his shoulder. Then he went on stacking his chips.

"A few years, off and on," he said. "Fortune, isn't it?"

"You remember," I said. "Why did you pick him and Ryan to help handle Bradley's escape for your brother?"

"The only Mexican crook I knew, and he wanted money. I never met Ryan before." He finished stacking the chips. "I don't know why they were killed, if that's what you really want to know. Adelita wanted to go back to Mexico with him. A favor for both of them. A nice favor, yes?"

His speech was disjointed, halting, like a record that was turning too slowly. As if he had something on his mind that kept intruding into his train of thought, making him forget for a second what he had been going to say next.

"Laura wants you to come home," I said.

"Does she?" He looked up again. "You've been seeing her, Fortune?"

"We've talked."

"Perhaps more? I wouldn't blame her."

"Who would?" I said.

He nodded, but I had lost him. A new hand was being dealt, and he leaned forward to follow the cards.

"Go home before you go to Mexico," I said.

"Mexico?" He almost looked up at me again, but he saw his hole cards first. Both kings. "Yes, I will."

He would go home, except that he had already forgotten what he'd said yes to. His hands putting the kings down gently, his whole thin body like a taut wire and fighting to look casual.

"Deal me out a few hands," Dutch Stahl said, nodded to me.

I followed him to a corner away from the table. I told him all I'd learned on the boat.

"They want me to go to Mexico with them."

"He was going to help an escape? Nestor?"

"For good money. And just help to 'arrange' an escape, not much risk probably," I said. "It seems Adelita was right, he was getting a stake so they could set up shop in Mexico."

The corner of Stahl's mouth twitched, and he suddenly sat down on a couch. No one can hide from anguish inside forever. The shell has to crack sometime, bend a little, at least for a moment. Across the room the cards went around and the game droned on. Stahl looked at me, looked toward the game, looked out the high windows at the gray November city with the storm moving in again, and looked back at me.

"All she ever had was a half-crazy dream of some cavalier on a white horse who would give her everything she wanted. She never thought she was anything herself, just ugly and worthless. So she lived in a dream world, an illusion." His flat, cool old eyes stared toward the six gamblers intent on nothing but cards going around and around. "We all have our illusions, don't we? To keep going, to beat time. For me it's keeping moving, never stay long anywhere. No roots, no home, no past, no obligations. Just keep moving from town to town, game to game, and the future is endless, time never catches up. Motion makes me immortal. That's my illusion."

"If it works, why not?"

He shook his head. "It worked for me, but not for Addie. An old con man with fast hands and wandering feet to keep time away. But Addie wanted a place, a name, something to be. She wanted it all roses and song. I couldn't give it to her, and neither could her mother, and she couldn't give it to herself, never had any respect for herself. Like Kern over there. That's why he has to gamble, and why she needed Nestor. The English writer, Thomas Hardy, he said it—life is a brief passage through a sorry world. I keep moving one day at a time, Kern runs and gambles, and Addie had to have a man to make her feel she was something."

It was more than he'd said the whole time I'd known him. Talking it out, killing the pain inside with words. We all do it, one way or another.

"You know anything about this Joe Ryan?" I said. "Did Nestor ever mention him?"

"I never heard of him." Stahl looked toward the darkening sky outside the windows again. "How was Nestor going to handle the escape down there?"

"I don't know. Probably with bribes."

"Or maybe a deal?" Stahl said. "You said he was a paid informer. Maybe he had someone to give the Mexican cops. A friend. That would be Nestor's style."

"It might explain those gunmen. Except they weren't Mexican."

Stahl thought. "I've heard that a lot of rebels from other Latin countries hide out in Mexico."

It was something worth thinking about.

"Will you go with them?" Stahl said.

"If those *pistoleros* didn't kill Nestor and Adelita, the key is Bradley Kern. There's a lot happening around him, and no one seems sure why he went to Mexico in the first place."

"Be careful," Stahl said. "It could be more dangerous than you know."

"Meaning?"

"Maybe Nestor made a different deal. Took the money to arrange the escape, then turned around and sold the boy and the escape plan to the Mexican cops." His cool eyes studied me. "Maybe the boy's friends sent those gunmen, or killed Nestor and Addie themselves. One of them, or all of them."

I could think about that, too. It fitted Cebellos. Did it fit one of the others? And which one?

"Bill Kern's supposed to go too," I said.

"He'd better lose then, or he won't move easy."

"Unless something else is pushing him this time."

I left Dutch Stahl heading back to his seat and the game. He would take care of Bill Kern's losing, and if I was going to Mexico, I had things to do.

One of them was to clean my old cannon. This time I would carry a gun.

19

We landed in San Antonio after dark. A rented car and pickup were waiting at the airport, and I saw little of the historic old city, and less of the dark countryside as we drove southwest toward Eagle Pass and the border.

Craig drove the car, with Luz Cebellos beside him. I got a nap in the back seat. Ryan and Bill Kern followed us in the pickup. On the jet Bill Kern had still had that hint of a smile at the corners of his thin mouth, the glow of the winner in his eyes. Relaxed with an aura of satisfaction. He wasn't a man to leave a game while he was winning. Not without some powerful pressure, or fear. Some extreme necessity, or maybe the promise of a lot more money to gamble with tomorrow.

Dawn and Eagle Pass arrived together, the silent farms and cattle fields stretching on all sides. The outskirts of the town were just beginning to stir as Craig pulled into a large motel. The fertile fields and scattered houses reached north, south and west, and in the distance the Rio Grande glistened in patches through the trees.

Craig had reserved a room for Luz, and a double suite for the rest of us. Ryan and Bill Kern went off somewhere in the pickup. Luz went to her room.

"You and I better get some sleep," Craig said.

I thought it was a good idea.

■ ■ ■

The voices talked out in the living room of the suite. Sun was high beyond my drawn shades. I lay on the bed in the thick air of all midday motel rooms, and listened to the voices. Tom Craig and Luz.

"You made all the contacts? Two men?"

"Everything the way you said," Luz's voice said.

"What about those gunmen? Any word about their friends, anyone else interested in Bradley?"

"Nothing I could find out."

There was a silence. Someone moved out there, and something clinked. Ice in glasses. Water ran. I reached for a cigarette, lit it, lay smoking in the translucent sunlight.

"You're sure you weren't involved with Nestor? Part of it before now?" Craig said quietly. "Perhaps with the gunmen?"

"I'm sure," Luz said. The ice clinked. She was drinking.

Craig was drinking, ice in two glasses. "So am I. With those gunmen in Fortune's office you were on his side, and Nestor never mentioned you."

"I was on my side, I always am. Nestor and I never had much to say to each other, or about each other."

Cars passed out on the highway, and I could hear distant voices across the fields. I smoked in the stuffy bedroom, and could picture them out in the living room drinking and watching each other. Like soldiers waiting for a dawn attack.

"I have twelve brothers and sisters," Luz's voice said. Low and detached, as if she sat out there with her eyes closed. "My father is a farmer in Morelos. Zapata fought to give us our own land, and we got it, but no one got enough to support themselves, so we still work for the hidalgos today. My oldest brother is a peon, my oldest sister is a maid married to a gardener for a wealthy family. The other children are still at home, barefoot and eating beans. Nestor and I got out, the hopes of the family. We came to America to make our fortunes and send money home. Nestor took more than he gave."

"And you?" Craig said.

The ice clinked. "I was a bright little girl. A local politician who wanted to seem benevolent and a friend of the people sent me to a special school. Eventually I was granted an exchange scholarship to USC. An honor and a favor to my parents, a free education and a glorious future." Her small laugh was ironic. "Of course they had to give me some money for food and clothes, and they lost the money I would have earned as a maid or fieldworker, or maybe a prostitute if I were pretty enough. But I became an educated woman, a great pride. Their great hope." The ice rattled again. "Educated to do nothing. A lot of knowledge, and no market value. They had to have money at home, I had to help. So I learned how to make money and live with my own in a country that doesn't really want an overeducated Mexican girl. I learned to make money any way I could, take money from where I could. Even from Nestor if I could grab it from him."

A silence stretched out there. Somewhere in the elegant motel a woman giggled and some men laughed. Incongruous, all of us waiting in an ordinary motel full of salesmen and lovers for the time to cross the border and arrange an escape.

"On the boat, you liked that squall," Craig's voice said. "I watched you. Up in the bow when we ran in. Action."

"What else is there?"

"What do you want, Luz? From life?"

"All I can get. Everything."

Craig laughed. "Who doesn't?"

"Most people don't," Luz said. "It scares them. It can be dangerous to want too much. Exposed, a risk. Afraid to lose."

"You're not afraid? Of losing, or maybe of winning?"

"No."

"The power? The top? All the way or nothing?"

"Power and money." Another silence. "I expect Fortune has told you I'm a sometime call girl? Or Bill Kern has."

"Bill probably never even noticed, he has other vices," Craig said. "Fortune doesn't talk much. He listens. I'm never sure what he's thinking, or what he knows. In a way I like that, and he can be useful."

"Is that what I am?" Luz said. "Useful?"

"I hope so," Craig said.

This time in the silence I could picture them looking at each other. They moved, the glasses were put down, and the door opened and closed.

I lay on the bed, not even sure myself what I was thinking.

░ ░ ░

Craig and I ate in the suite. Soon after dark, Ryan arrived with Luz and a small, dark Mexican man. Bill wasn't there. Craig took me into a bedroom.

"We have to get a message to Bradley. That's why you're here. I want you to memorize the message, and go over into Piedras Negras. That Mexican will take you, the visit's all arranged. You deliver the message, and come straight back."

I nodded. "Give me the message."

"Tell him—his mother asked you to visit him tonight. She wants him to know that his friend Ryan and his wife hope to see him soon, and that she'll be sending two packages for him. She hopes he's doing what they ask, and being careful."

"That's it?"

"Word for word, you understand?"

Instructions for Brad Kern—in code so that what I didn't know I couldn't tell. We went over it until I had it. Then the silent Mexican drove me into Eagle Pass and across the international bridge into the darker sprawl of Piedras Negras.

░ ░ ░

He was a miniature replica of his father. The same soft, boyish heaviness in the Mexican prison garb, but four inches shorter and with his mother's dark hair. The round, friendly face was haggard, and his father's pale blue eyes didn't blend as well with the dark hair. Juvenile eyes without that sense of authority Wallace Kern had. His voice was low.

"Who are you?"

They had searched me, and then left us alone. Different countries have different ways.

"Dan Fortune. Tom Craig and your father sent me."

I had waited some time to finally meet him, and I studied him. He was nervous, uneasy. But not as if he were afraid. Apologetic, as if he knew he was causing a great deal of trouble for a lot of people.

"How is my father?" he said.

"Worried."

"Is he . . . over there? With Tom?"

"No. Brad? Did you come down here to do something that got you into this? Are you guilty of something?"

"No!" His voice rose and cracked. He turned away. "I'm guilty of nothing. They hammered at me for three weeks. Naked on a bed, strapped down, a gun at my head! They had a confession—all in Spanish. Three weeks, over and over. So I signed it, and they gave me fifteen years!"

"Why *did* you come down here?"

"A visit! That's all. A vacation."

"Anna Botha doesn't think so."

"Anna?" In the dim cell he brightened for a moment. Then he shook his head. "She's wrong. She doesn't know anything."

There was an edge of bitterness in his voice. A cloud on the innocence of those blue eyes that dominated his juvenile face. The pale, almost bottomless eyes of Nordic fanatics. Of a Galahad, a Parsifal, a Nathan Hale, ready to cleanse the world with one brave, pure act that would make everything perfect. Or was I only thinking of what Anna Botha had said about him?

"Who killed Nestor Cebellos and Adelita Stahl?"

"Killed?" The boyish face frowned. "Who are they?"

"You never knew Nestor Cebellos? Maybe Joe Ryan?"

"I never heard of them!"

There was no reason he should have, not if he'd had no connection to them before he was jailed.

"Tell me about the Bolivian rebel guerillas."

"B . . . Bol . . . Bolivian? I . . . I don't know anything about Bolivian rebels! Why should I?"

Too much, too strong. He did know something about those gunmen, or about Bolivia. But before or after he was jailed?

"Who sent you down here, Brad? Your mother? Sam Tower? Bill Kern? Your father? Who?"

"I came on a visit! A vacation!" He was almost panting now, glaring at me in the silent cell. "Why are you asking all these questions? Tom Craig didn't send you here to ask me questions! What are you here for?"

I heard footsteps coming toward us. My time was nearly up.

"They sent a message: Your mother asked me to visit you tonight. She wants you to know that your friend Ryan and his wife hope to see you soon, and that she'll be sending two packages for you. She hopes you're doing what they ask, and being careful. That's it. You understand?"

He smiled at me, and nodded. Eagerness in his pale eyes.

The Mexican guards led me out. An officer walked beside me through the dim and dingy prison toward the entrance.

"You are a close friend of young Kern?" His English was good. "A sad affair, we much regret it."

"Fifteen years is a long time for a small crime."

"Small?" He watched me. "Perhaps that is a matter of opinion. I am afraid Americans do not accept our justice."

"We think it's a little harsh."

"Perhaps. We are a simpler people. Justice here must be clear and simple. Direct. We do not always understand American ways."

"Maybe we can all try," I said.

We reached the street. Dark and empty, a glow to the north showing where the border was. Another country.

"Did you know, Mr. Fortune, that Mexican prisoners in your jails also hate it? They wish to come home to our prisons? It seems that people even prefer their own ethnic punishment."

It leaves us all with a long way to go. Even me. As we drove back across the bridge over the silver shine of the Rio Grande, I felt a weight lift. Home.

20

Only Ryan was in the motel suite. The big man sat at a table in his boots and field jacket, the red beret trim and square on his head, cleaning an M-16 automatic rifle. His powerful hands worked fast and delicately. Trained and experienced.

I lay on the couch. "Where'd you get the beret?"

"Africa," Ryan said, not looking up. "Limey paratrooper."

"You served with the British?"

"No."

I lit a cigarette. "Where in Africa?"

"Anywhere." He looked up. "Where they paid me."

I didn't pursue it. A mercenary. It had been written all over him from the start, from that day in the park. The knife in my back and the quick, sure skill.

"Where else besides Africa? South America?"

"Asia. They don't use mercenaries in South America."

"Trained in Mexico sometime?"

"Hell, no. I never been to Mexico before now. They got no use for hired soldiers. Not yet, anyway."

"Where'd you meet Nestor Cebellos?"

He wiped oil from the receiver. "Around."

"In New York?"

"Yeh, in New York."

He finished the rifle, slammed the bolt home, wiped it all clean, and laid it aside on the table. The knife was in his boot. He took it out, tested the point and edge and strength against the table, and returned it to its boot sheath. He began to work on a .45 automatic pistol. A man who took care of his tools. Lived by them.

"How'd it start, Ryan?" I smoked.

He worked. "You got a lot of questions."

"Sorry. Passing time. Never did like waiting."

On the couch I closed my eyes. I waited. Ryan had probably spent most of his life in one army or another, many years as a soldier for pay, and mercenaries learn to do their job and say little. Soldiers in all armies learn silence in a crowd. But men who live alone, the crowd gone, need to talk to someone sooner or later. A conflict Ryan would have to work out for himself. No army around, and waiting gets to everyone.

"You got to learn how to wait," Ryan said. He oiled the trigger mechanism of the automatic. "The Marines. Viet Nam. Joined out of high school. I never was any good in school, had no trade, hated offices. I liked the Marines, took to soldiering like a big-assed duck. Combat." His eyes seemed to glow in the motel room. "You lose that arm in the war?"

"Merchant marine. I'm no soldier."

He nodded, worked on the pistol clip. "Most guys ain't got it. Not in the Corps even, and not in the jungles. You gotta be born with it, the liking fighting. I seen guys in all the mercenary outfits crying to go home. We even had to shoot some. Crazies, cowards, poor bastards come down because they got to have the big money but didn't have the guts to make it. I remember this guy in the jungle was out on—"

"Why did you leave the Marines?"

He worked the slide of the automatic. "Was in a good outfit, the best. They broke us up. My time was up, so I walked out. Stupid. No one soldiers like the Corps."

"But you joined mercenaries? Any army better than none?"

He tested the pistol, clicked on an empty chamber. He holstered the automatic, sat back.

"I walked the street for a year. Stateside. Fights and whores." In the chair he moved, restless. A giant of a man in the castoff clothes of three armies. "I walk around, and most days I can't remember. I walk in a suit and tie, and they all pass, the weeks and months, and it's like nothing touches me. I go through a town and there ain't a mark on me nowhere to say I been there. Nothing to do, nowhere to go."

"But you ran out of armies, came to New York? Cebellos had a job for good pay."

Ryan nodded. "I came to New York."

"You think those gunmen killed him? Cebellos?"

"I ain't sure. I guess so."

Dr. Tom Craig stood in the doorway. "It's time."

     ▦   ▦   ▦

Craig drove the pickup fast through the night. From time to time a river glistened to the left through trees.

"Where are we going?" I asked.

"You'll see. Not too far."

"Just the two of us?"

"The others will be along."

Half an hour later Craig turned off the highway into a narrow, shadowy dirt road to the left. He drove slowly ahead on the dirt road until it dipped down into a broad river bed with a narrow stream flowing out in the center like a silver ribbon. Craig drove across the river bed, slowly fording the shallow stream, and up into another dirt road on the far side. At the edge of another blacktop highway he parked the truck in a grove of cottonwoods, and sat back.

"We've got a little wait," he said.

I looked around in the dark night. The only lights were back on the other side of the river. Scattered houses. On this side there was nothing. Only the empty highway.

"What was that river?" I said.

"The Rio Grande," Craig said. "You didn't guess?"

I'd guessed. We were in Mexico. And not legally.

"You'd better tell me now," I said.

Craig watched me. "When Wally asked me for help, I said there was only one way—direct action. Bribes and deals are no good, you can't trust other people. There was only one sure way to free Bradley."

"A jailbreak. That's why you needed Ryan, a soldier. Ryan, Luz, and that Mexican are breaking Brad out of that jail at two A.M. tonight. The message."

"They're well armed, they'll take the jail by surprise, free Bradley and any other American who wants to escape." He smiled in the night. "The Mexicans will expect Ryan to head for Eagle Pass. They'll block the bridge, watch the river. But Ryan will stay in Mexico and drive here. He'll send the others he breaks out straight for the river. They'll make good decoys. We abandon the car, go back through those shallows. The Americans won't like it all much either, so we don't go back to Eagle Pass. Bill is waiting in a safe hideout north and west."

"Decoys? The other Americans?"

"Most will escape. Necessity can be hard."

In the dark of the truck cab his eyes seemed to have a light of their own.

"You like this, don't you? The action, the challenge. You need it."

"I enjoy action, Fortune, I don't need it. When you need something, you always lose."

"Does that go for needing people, too?"

"Especially for people. The one who needs the other least always dominates a relationship."

"Who is it with you and Marjorie Kern?"

His laugh sent small animals scurrying in the brush. "So you spotted that, did you? I thought you would. I'm not sure who needs who the least. She's a fairly shallow woman, but I suppose it's me. I find her pleasant, but not a lot more, and she knows that. That's why she wanted to hire you, I think. She saw that I was busy with something secret outside the office, and I suspect she wanted you to find out what it was so she would have a hold on me. She didn't realize then that I was working for Wally and Brad, wanted some power over me."

"No problem that she's Wallace's wife? A friend?"

"She chased me, and I'm not the first. Wally knows her, but he doesn't know how to handle her. It was her choice, I never enticed her. And I'm not sure how much longer she'll last with Wally. From either side."

"You're sure she wanted me to report on you? That's all?"

"No, I'm not sure." That careful judgment. "Aren't you?"

"I don't think Brad came down here on his own. She could be behind his trip, or maybe Sam Tower."

"Sam?"

I told him what I knew about Sam Tower's nosing around. About Fred Sarguis.

"So that explains who searched Wally's desk," Craig said slowly. "Fred Sarguis wouldn't miss any chance to make a dollar or gain an advantage. I'll have to talk to Brad."

"About more than Sarguis," I said. "I think he knows something about those Bolivian gunmen."

He said nothing to that. Only moved in the cab to look out at the dark night. Maybe thinking about Bolivia and his days of action at the jungle hospital.

"Why did you come back from South America?" I said.

"The government threw me out. I told you."

"It hadn't stopped you before. Government opposition."

He went on watching the night and the deserted road. "I suppose the challenge was over, becoming routine. I had my work up here. I'm a scientist as well as a doctor, you can't make advances down there treating Indians. You have to be an expert to move on today, to build and change. What happened down there was a necessity, it had to be done, and I was the only one who could do it. But I had my own work up here. I was needed here."

"By science? To do important work?"

"Yes. I think so."

"I wonder if you weren't more important down there? I'm not sure any of us are needed much singly. The value of life is to work for everyone, the group. The way Anna Botha says."

"Communal value only?" He turned to me, his face in shadow. "Perhaps. It's an interesting thought, anyway. In a different time and place I could have thought like that, I suppose. Time is all important." He turned his head to watch the night once more. "Only time happens to men, history to societies, chemistry to worlds. A man has to work when and where he is."

"Is that the scientist, or the man of action?"

"Both, I think," and he laughed again.

The animals that scurried to his laugh this time weren't small. Large shapes moving heavily through the brush and, suddenly, along the road.

"Here they are!" Craig opened the cab door.

I didn't move. There were too many. Crashing through the brush all around us. Running up along the road. In uniforms. With guns.

A light pinned us.

A Mexican officer walked toward the truck with his pistol out and an angry face.

21

Not a jail. A bare adobe storeroom, flour sacks piled on the dirt floor. Dawn outside the barred window, and the gray houses and dirt streets were not in Piedras Negras.

"Why here?" I said. "Why not some real jail?"

Through the glassless window I watched chickens scratch in the dust. A rooster crowed somewhere. In the dim dawn, burned brown hills stretched into an endless distance.

"Someone turned us in," Craig said.

He sat across the room on a pile of sacks against the wall. His face showed nothing, and he hadn't moved from the wall since they'd thrown us in here hours ago. Nerveless.

"You can't be sure," I said. "Some mistake. They could have been picked up on their way to us, and the Mexicans guessed they'd have someone waiting at that ford."

"Then they've got us cold," he said, "but I don't think that happened. No reason to suspect more raiders waiting."

I didn't think so either. Then who? Brad Kern had been nervous, hiding something. Luz was a Cebellos.

"Ryan fights for anyone who pays," I said. "Someone could have paid him better first. To fight with those rebels."

"We'll find out," Craig said.

We didn't have long to wait. The sun was barely up when the wooden door flung open. A swarthy soldier came in with a chair. He set it down, dusted it with a cloth, and stood at attention. A thin officer strode in and sat down. The same officer who had captured us.

"To break a jail is very bad. Many bad prisoners escape." His English had a heavy accent. "Many swim the river, we know that. One was taken by the car, by the criminals. You were to meet the criminals, yes? You are not there. Where do the criminals go when you are not there to meet?"

The escape had succeeded! Bradley Kern had gone with Ryan, Luz and the Mexican in the car. Then how had the Mexicans known we were waiting? Craig saw it as soon as I did. With me, and ahead of me. If the escape had succeeded, then . . .

"Jailbreak?" Craig said. "What jailbreak? We know nothing about a jailbreak. We were meeting no one. Mr. Fortune and I were visiting Mexico. We came across at Del Rio, were driving to Piedras Negras."

"At night? The side of the road is Piedras Negras?"

Craig was calm. "We crossed in daylight. But we were foolish and left the highway. We became lost. When we found the highway again it was very late. We were tired, we stopped to rest. It is dangerous to drive when you are tired."

The officer glared at us. I watched him. I'd realized what Craig had—if the escape had succeeded, how had they known where we were and why? Even if they knew, what proof could they have if everyone had escaped? The officer stood up.

"You will come."

He turned his back, and the swarthy soldier herded us out after him. We were in some old adobe hacienda. The officer stalked into a large, low main room with windows that faced north from the angle of the sunrise. The soldier pushed us to stand at the windows beside the officer who pointed to a distant line of trees, and a tall church steeple beyond the trees.

"You see that tower? That is the United States. Your country, yes? It is so near, yes? But there is between us a wall. Yes, a wall you cannot see, but it is as high as the mountains. It is higher! A wall to the sky. A wall you cannot climb. You are here. You will be here very long. A million miles from that tower, from your country! Unless you tell—"

The man who came in wore civilian clothes. Good clothes. A neat dark suit and tie. A small man, but the officer paled as he saw him and came stiffly to attention.

"*Generale!* I did not—"

"Leave us alone, Captain," the small man said, and nodded at the soldier. "That one too. Take him with you."

The officer and the soldier went out hastily. With a sigh, the small man looked after them as the door closed. He shook his head, almost to himself, and turned to us.

"We love titles too much, the glory of rank. One of our weaknesses. Think of me as a simple policeman with a problem." He waved to some chairs. "Sit down, Dr. Craig, Mr. Fortune."

We sat down. He sat facing us. He smiled.

"A famous scientist, and a detective from New York. I have not been in New York for many years. It has changed?"

"Not much," I said. "Details."

"Great cities change slowly." He nodded. "So, you arranged a jail-break. A skillful action, I admire your choice of personnel. And your loyalty, Dr. Craig. Your employer's son. Then, what else would be expected of Dr. Tom Craig?"

"What jailbreak?" I said.

"You're confusing us, sir," Craig said. "Are you saying that you no longer hold Bradley Kern in prison? An escape?"

"Come, Doctor, we know that you and Fortune—"

Craig was up. "An escape? You expect us to believe that? If anything happens, or has happened, to Bradley Kern, you and your government won't get away with any trumped-up story—!"

"Sit down, Dr. Craig!" the small man snapped. "So, you know that the escape succeeded. From Captain Orantes, I expect. He always was an idiot. Well, no matter."

"We don't know what you may have heard, or why you arrested us," Craig said, "but you can't prove we had any connection—"

"I have said it does not matter. We have no intention of charging you. I did not come for that. The world-famous Dr. Tom Craig? No way, as you say across the border."

"What did you come for?" I said.

"I hope to help us all," the small man said. "We found you through a telephone call from your side of the border half an hour after the raid. If we wanted the raiders, we must go to Ciudad Acuna-Piedras Negras highway near Comanche Bend."

"No names?" I said. "No details?"

"No," the Mexican said. "It had to be one of the raiders, young Kern himself, or some associate you are perhaps not aware of yourselves. Assuming that you know anything." He got up, began to pace with his hands behind him. "We know that Mr. Wallace Kern believes his son innocent of any charge, made all efforts to release him, legal and illegal. We are aware of a certain Nestor Cebellos and his bribery. We allowed Cebellos to do his work."

"Allowed?" Craig said.

"We wanted whoever else might have been involved with young Kern. Unfortunately, your . . . the raid surprised us. We had not expected that. Perhaps we should have."

"Involved with Brad Kern in what?" I asked.

"Smuggling and selling drugs."

"Ridiculous!" Tom Craig snapped. "Bradley never used drugs in his life, certainly wouldn't have smuggled any into the United States. He hates that kind of dirty greed."

"An idealist? Yes," the small man said, "and that helps to confirm our charge. There is another kind of drug, isn't there?"

"Medicine," I said.

He nodded. "Antibiotics to be exact, and not smuggled into *your* country, but into *ours*. He brought an illegal shipment of antibiotics into Mexico, and sold them illegally."

Somewhere outside the low room of the hacienda the Mexican soldiers were drilling. A ragged tramp of feet in the dust, the hoarse and furious snarls of the noncoms. All armies.

"Sold?" I said. "Bradley Kern? An idealist?"

"It is possible the boy was duped, we think he was. But he brought the antibiotics across the border in a truck by night, and they were sold."

"Why bring them here, take the risk of smuggling? Why not just sell them in the States? Legally?"

"Because he could not, Mr. Fortune. The risk would have seemed even greater." He sat down again, lit a small cigar. "International trade is complicated and political, yes? The antibiotics were sold to a political refugee group allowed in Mexico, but not in the United States. It is a Federal offense to sell to them in the States, illegal for them even to be in the States. A CIA and FBI matter." He smoked the small cigar slowly. "We allow the refugees political asylum in Mexico, it must have seemed best to make the sale here, and there could be great profit in such a black-market sale."

"Was it so bad?" I said. "Medicines? Even for a profit?"

"We permit the refugees to live here, Mr. Fortune, but not to operate. It could create a grave problem for us."

"A political problem," Craig said. "A boy like Bradley thinks in terms of human problems, not politics."

"Pure acts for a perfect world, Dr. Craig?" the small Mexican said. "An innocent? Not realizing that few are pure, and fewer even want a perfect world. They simply want to own what there is."

I sensed it—he was holding something back.

"These refugees he sold the drugs to. Bolivians?"

"Yes. A Bolivian rebel group."

"The gunmen?" Craig said.

The small man said nothing. He looked away from us toward an empty corner of the low room. Outside, the soldiers tramped on through the dust.

I said, "Bradley sold them medicine they probably needed desperately in the jungle, yet they were chasing anyone who might have been involved with him, and they called him a murderer. They were full of hate and anger."

The General smoked. "Some weeks ago a report reached us. Unofficial, but more than a rumor, and very reliable. The shipment of antibiotics was sent to the jungles safely, and they were used." He looked at each of us. "Used, and many died. The shipment was defective. Useless, and worse. Either simply substandard, or contaminated, or . . . adulterated."

He sat there as silent as we did.

"What did Bradley tell you?" I said.

"He would not speak."

"You told him about the bad drugs?"

"No. We felt it best not to, how do you say, tip our hand?" He leaned forward, tapped out the small cigar. "There is much sympathy in Mexico for the Bolivian rebels. After the tragic report, someone informed them of the efforts to free young Kern, of the bribes of Cebellos on his behalf. This I regret, but I can understand why it was done."

The link and the motive. I'd have wanted to kill Cebellos too. Or would I have? Alive, he could have told me all.

"I said I came to help us all," the small General said. "We want whoever is responsible, we think that you do too. The escape has taken it out of our hands, so we decided to tell you all we knew. If young Kern was duped, he may be in far greater danger now than in our prison. If he was not duped, knew what he did, then others may be in danger."

"General?" I said. "Do you know a Joe Ryan?"

"Ryan?" He thought. "I think I do not."

I stood up. "Can we go?"

"Captain Orantes will return your pistol, Mr. Fortune." He stood up too. "I have a feeling that you may need it. It is clear that someone did not want you to be with Bradley Kern."

*　*　*

By noon we were fifty miles north of Del Rio on a back highway. Craig drove the pickup hard. We had said little.

"Where's the rendezvous?" I said as we drove on.

"Rocksprings," Craig said. "Near it."

"Nothing is missing from Kern Labs."

"There are other companies. Anyone at Kern can get drugs."

"Who?" I said. "Who needs money that badly?"

He said nothing. Soon signs began to announce the distance to Rocksprings. Craig drove faster.

"They won't be there, Craig," I said. "The General was right. That call set us up so they could get away without us. To give someone time."

"Bill could be there," Craig said. "Know something."

A mile this side of Rocksprings he turned off into a dirt road. It was a ramshackle farmhouse. There was no car. We went inside. The food left there was untouched. The beds had not been used. Dust still covered the floor. No one was there, not even Bill Kern. No one had been there. Craig looked around.

"I sent Bill to wait here," he said. "Before the raid."

"He never made it."

"Or didn't try."

We drove on toward Austin.

22

November rain dripped from the big house in the early night. Light blazed from all the downstairs windows, but there were no cars in the long drive that curved beyond the wide lawn. Craig rang. Rang again.

"Well come in!" A woman's voice, loud and harsh.

The broad entry hall was alight. In the empty living room every light was on. There was no one in the bright dining room. She was in the den. Marjorie Kern. Alone, all the lights on, the TV blaring, a drink in her hand. A serious drink.

"You're alone?" Craig said.

"Alone." She drank, looked at me. "You're not."

"Why all the lights?" I said.

"I like light! It's Saturday night. I like fun. I like to spend money. I hate rain. I hate maids who get sick!"

"Where's Wallace?" Craig asked.

"Who knows?" She drank. "Out. Gone."

"Gone?" I said. "How long has he been gone? Where is he? Was he out last night?"

"I don't know where he was last night. I don't care."

"You don't know if he was home last night?" I said.

She laughed. "I don't know because *I* wasn't home last night. All night. Wild!"

"Where were you, Marjorie?" Craig said.

"I didn't know you cared, *Mister* Craig. Off on your important mission. I was around and about. On the town. Having fun. Celebrating!" She drained her drink, looked at it, and then sat down. She looked at Craig. "I had it out, Tom. With Wallace. We had it out once and for all.

Thursday night after we were on the boat. He was going to a meeting that night, he was going to be away on business all day Friday. No time for me! I couldn't stand it any longer, so I told him!"

"Wallace had a meeting Thursday night?" I said. "Away on business all day Friday? What business? Where?"

"I don't know. In New York. Some business."

Craig said, "What did you tell him, Marjorie?"

"About us! You and me. He knew, really, had guessed, but I told him anyway!"

"What about us, Marjorie?" Craig said.

"Everything! That we love each other. Our plans."

"Plans?" Craig said. "My plans are at Kern Labs. My work. You know that." He crossed the study to a small bar, began to mix a scotch and water. "What did he say?"

"Say? Wallace? He said I was stupid. That's all. Stupid! Nothing about love, about me and him, about wanting *me*. " She held out her glass. Craig took it, mixed a scotch for her. "So we had it out, Tom, the whole thing. I told him we were through, even without you. I can't stand it anymore. He *likes* his life. He likes Connecticut, his work, his house. He feels dedicated to the Labs, he wants to do a *good job*. Nothing about making a lot of money, and what else is there? Why else do you work?"

"A lot of reasons, Marjorie," Craig said.

"Not for me! I want to live, have everything I can get and more. I want to move, go places, do things. With you, Tom. You're a brilliant man, powerful. You can make millions, work anywhere. You can be important, and I want to be with you."

Craig handed her the drink. She sat looking up at him, watching his face. He smiled, bent and kissed her. She clung to his neck. They were like that a long minute. Then Craig took her hands away, straightened up.

"You make it sound exciting," he said. "Why not?"

"It will be, Tom, I promise you. Oh, I told him at last. I'm finished with him! I went out to celebrate. The truth."

"All night?" I said.

"What?" She turned to me. "Shocked, Mr. Fortune?"

"Can you name the places? Did anyone see you?"

"Perhaps, I don't know. Just taverns, bars. Why?"

Craig said, "We freed Bradley last night. Broke him out of that jail. But we lost him again."

"Bradley's free? Safe?"

"Free," I said, "I don't know how safe." I explained what had happened in Mexico. I told her about the drugs. "We were set up by someone. Can you prove you were in Connecticut?"

"Me? You think I went to Mexico?"

"What taverns, Marjorie," Craig said. "For Fortune."

"All of them near here! I'm known. People saw me." She glared at both of us. Then she smiled. First at me, then at Craig. "He is safe, isn't he? You don't really think he's still in danger?"

"Or in hiding," I said.

"Because he sold bad drugs? Bradley? Never!"

"Then he's in danger. One or the other," I said.

She seemed to think about it. She shook her head. "No, he's fine. If he's free, he's all right. He's just gone off somewhere without telling you. He's always done that. What you think happened in Mexico was some kind of mistake." She smiled to Craig. "We have to think about us, Tom."

I thought of Laura Kern. Marjorie wouldn't stand by a paperhanger, or anyone with a problem. It wasn't that she was unconcerned for her son, but that she wouldn't, or couldn't, think of anything except herself unless tragedy hit her in the face. Only immediate trouble could turn her attention from her own needs. Unless she knew more than we did about Bradley.

"We can wait, Marjorie," Craig said. "Drugs were sold, Bradley has vanished."

"I won't listen! Bradley could never have—"

I said, "Maybe he didn't know what he was doing. The Mexicans don't think he did it alone. Maybe he thought he was doing something else."

"You mean. . . . You mean someone fooled him? Used him?" She looked up at Craig. "Who? Tom?"

"That's what we have to find out," Craig said.

She held her drink in both hands. She had it now. But she still didn't want it. She wanted Tom Craig and the big life.

"You haven't seen Wallace since Thursday night?" I said.

"No. He's been gone since early Friday." She swirled her scotch. "But Anna Botha called here today asking for him. More than once. Perhaps she reached him somewhere."

* * *

The three-story frame house was in New Canaan. Anna Botha had the top floor. She answered the door. Trim in black slacks and a white blouse against her brown skin, the beautiful face set in tight lines, looking over our shoulders.

"Is he here? Bradley?"

"No," I said.

We went in. African masks on the walls, a Zulu shield with two assagais, faded photographs of old warriors, a large map of South Africa. The study lined with books, in English and Afrikaans. Native stools, tables, jugs in the living room. The bedroom door closed.

"But you freed him?"

"We freed him," I said, "and lost him." I told her what had happened in Texas and Mexico.

"Then he *is* still in danger?"

"From someone, we think," Craig said. "Where were you the last few days, Anna?"

Had Craig heard the inflection, too? *Then he* is *still in danger?* As if she had, somehow, known already that Brad might be in danger? Heard it? Dreamed it?

Her full lips set hard. "You think I would sell death to Bolivian peasants, Dr. Craig? Look at me. Am I someone who makes money from the enslaved, joins the generals?"

"Whites aren't the only ones who want money," Craig said.

I said, "You're someone Bradley would listen to, Anna. Someone he'd trust without asking any questions."

"He'd do that with Dr. Craig there, too. With anyone he trusted and believed in."

"But you most," Craig said. "First and most."

"I don't have to—!"

The bedroom door opened. Wallace Kern came out. His florid, fleshy face was sallow, tired. He looked like he had slept in his clothes, and hadn't slept well.

"Tell them, Anna," he said. "Tell them where you were."

The big company president sat down in a wicker armchair, leaned back against the high back, and covered his eyes with one soft hand. Anna Botha sat on the arm of the chair, put her hand on his shoulder, spoke without turning to us.

"All day Friday I worked in my laboratory. I worked late, went to bed early. Today I worked here on my book. Stories of my home, of people like the Bolivian Indians. Until—"

Wallace Kern uncovered his face. "Tell me again what happened down there, Fortune. Everything."

I told him again. Hour by hour.

"A phone call? Who? That Ryan we hired with Cebellos? The sister? Someone else?"

"Ryan is a mercenary," I said. "He fights for anyone who pays him. Someone could have paid him better than you did. Luz Cebellos wants money. As much or more than Nestor did."

"Bradley?"

I said nothing.

"Or even me? Not alone, I didn't know where you were anymore than Anna did. But perhaps with one of the others? Don't you want to know where I was?"

"Where were you, Wallace?" Craig said.

Toneless, like a robot, "I was at home on Thursday night with Marjorie. With my wife." For the first time he turned in the chair toward

Tom Craig. "We had a talk, my wife and I. I didn't sleep very well that night. On Friday I had a meeting in New York. I went to New York, but not to the meeting. I canceled the meeting, walked a lot. I came home late. My wife did not come home. I did not sleep well again. Today I drove my car. All day." His blue eyes fixed on Craig. "I had a lot to think about, didn't I, Tom? All day. Then I went to the office. There was a message from Anna. I came here."

Anna Botha had her hand on his neck, rubbed gently.

"Wallace," Craig said, "I'm not going to—"

"You're a lot alike, Tom, you and Marjorie. On the surface. She wants action, excitement, even risk. Alive. But she's a fake. There's no real strength. I'm sorry for her."

"I never enticed her," Craig said, "never promised—"

"Conscience? No need. If it wasn't you, then someone else. I was never really her kind of man. Too sober, too soft. I wonder how many millions of people marry the wrong kind of person?" Kern shook his head. "The odd part is she may really need my kind of man. An antagonist who'll put up with her."

Craig said, "You want her to stay with you, Wally?"

"No advice, all right?"

"Of course," Craig said. "You're too good for her, Wallace."

"No I'm not, Tom, but that's my problem. Marjorie is my problem not yours, not yet, and right now we have a more important problem." He glanced up at Anna Botha who was still rubbing his neck as if to comfort him. "Anna called me, and I came, because she had received a call—from Bradley."

Craig said, "A call? From where? Where is he!"

"When?" I said.

Anna Botha said, "Early this morning. From somewhere in Texas. He sounded uneasy, confused. He was with a man and a woman, on his way to meet Dr. Craig. Then he was cut off."

"At a gas station," Wallace Kern said. "When Anna told me, it scared me. Almost like he was a prisoner. I wondered where you two were, what was happening."

"We had a rendezvous," Craig said. "They never went. Are you sure he sounded confused, or just nervous? Running away."

"No," Anna said, "I'm not sure."

She went on rubbing Wallace Kern's neck. He hardly seemed to notice. Distracted.

"He sold a shipment of antibiotics," I said. "A whole truckload. Where did he get it?"

"Not from Kern Labs," Craig said. "We know that."

"Do we?" Wallace Kern said. He hunched forward in the chair. "Every ounce of our production is traceable, yes. Every *good* ounce. Every bad ounce is accounted for, Tom, but is it traceable?"

"Bad ounce?" I said.

"All companies have bad batches, Fortune. Contaminated, not up to specifications. They are destroyed in our incinerator. We log them out, truck them to the dump, log them in, and burn them. Our people see the batch leave the plant, but only the truck driver sees it delivered at the dump, and only the dump man sees it actually destroyed. Or he sees boxes go into the incinerator. He's not trained to tell what's in them."

I said, "How many truck drivers do you have?"

"Ten. I'll have security start checking them."

"You know what you're suggesting?" I said. "That someone *knew* the drugs were defective from the start. And sold them."

Anna Botha said, "Not Bradley."

"Tower?" Craig said, and he told them all I had told him about Sam Tower and Fred Sarguis. "Sarguis would do it."

"No, I can't believe it!" Wallace Kern said. "Not Sam. Not even Fred Sarguis. He's ruthless, but not—"

"We better talk to Tower," Craig said grimly.

Wallace Kern just sat there. Anna Botha rested her slim brown hand on his heavy shoulder, watched him.

"It couldn't be anyone who understood the horror of it," she said. "Not Bradley, Wallace. None of us. There has to be another answer."

"Your wife might not realize what it meant, Kern," I said.

His head jerked up. "Marjorie? You can't—!"

"Or," I said, "there's one other person who might not know the danger of bad drugs, and who would do almost anything for money. Someone Bradley would trust all the way, believe. The one who brought Cebellos and Ryan to you—Bill."

They were all silent. Then Craig nodded.

"The need, the opportunity, and he's missing too."

I turned for the door. "You find Tower. I'll look for Bill."

In the rain the small house behind the white fence was dark. I rang anyway, looked at my watch. Seven o'clock. Where was Laura? I used my keys.

There was nothing in the living room, dining room, kitchen or bathroom. Nothing in the bedroom. Silent and empty, cold and lonely in the steady rain.

I drove the rented car toward the city.

* * *

At the St. Charles Hotel the game was slow. Bill Kern wasn't there. Neither was Dutch Stahl. Someone thought Dutch was in a big East Side game. No one knew anything about Bill Kern.

"Where on the East Side?"

They told me.

The winter rain blew with me through the park.

* * *

It was a casino operation. Double doors, quiet rooms, and dinner jackets. Diamonds and professional dealers. Middle-aged muscle behind a desk in black tie. We'd met.

"You're a long way from Chelsea. Not your kind of action."

"I'm looking for a William Kern, and Arizona Dutch."

"The paperhanger?" He shook his head. "The door's closed, even with cash. We've been burned."

"Isn't it always made good?"

"The family? Mostly, not always, and it's trouble."

"You're not supposed to mind a little trouble."

"Disneyland. You know we don't like hustle and muscle. Not for peanuts. It got to be a real big nut before the heat's worth leaning on a mark. For small change we get burned, too."

"How about Dutch?"

"Why?"

"I'm working for him."

"On what?"

"His daughter's murder."

He nodded. "I heard. He was here, left with some farmers for a private game. West Side Health Spa."

Blowing east, the rain seemed to want to hold me in the park. Shadows along the black sheen of the drive waiting to come out, surround me, smile.

░ ░ ░

New York midtown streets are never deserted, but fewer people walked in the winter rain. The girls sheltered in doorways, walked under umbrellas, more insistent in the rain as on the streets of war-torn cities.

"Why the hell they want Luz?"

She was a brunette, short, too heavy.

"I wouldn't know," I said.

"Gay?"

"Poor," I said. "She's working?"

She was already looking for other prospects. The street offered thin pickings. She had some time.

"Ain't seen her in a couple o' days. Heard she was gone back to Mexico. Hope so, more for the rest of us. Not that she'd work the rain anyway."

She saw an opportunity approaching, walking nervous. She framed her best smile, moved in. I walked on.

At the West Side Health Spa the game was in a room next to the manager's office. Or it would be. After dinner. They had all gone to a restaurant down the street. I couldn't miss them.

I didn't. There were six of them at a big table. The restaurant was loud and frantic, a sporting crowd. Drinking, watching basketball, making bets, yelling.

Dutch Stahl sat alone at the bar, an empty sandwich plate and half a glass of beer in front of him. In a dark blue suit and tie, his shirt starched and his shoes shined. Reading a newspaper and sipping the beer as the bets and noise flowed around him. The next stool was empty. I sat down.

"You seen anything of Bill Kern?"

"Not since Thursday."

He nodded almost imperceptibly to the bartender and to me. I accepted a beer. Dutch ordered another. He held the second beer as if wondering what he was doing with it. I didn't think he had two beers before a game often.

"We always ate dinner together. Not other meals, but dinner. Whenever we could." He drank. "What happened in Mexico?"

I told him. He sat silent. Drank the beer.

"Antibiotics? That's what it was about? A bad shipment? This Kern kid, Nestor, and—Addie?"

"We're not sure Brad Kern knew it was a bad batch. Fooled. Adelita probably didn't know it was bad either."

"As good as murder. That's what he got her into this time? Addie? That's what got her killed?"

"It looks like it," I said.

He pushed the beer away. "You think there was someone else behind it? Working with that Kern and Nestor?"

"That's what we think. It could be Joe Ryan, or another person, or both."

"Who is Ryan?"

"A mercenary soldier Cebellos brought into the escape plan with him." I described the big mercenary.

"I've seen that man," Dutch said.

"With Cebellos?"

"No, in my hotel. I think I saw him talking to Addie."

"You did," I said. "She never mentioned him?"

He shook his head. "I wonder where Nestor met him? When? He doesn't sound like Nestor's type at all."

"They met here in New York."

"Here?" He folded his newspaper, glanced toward the table where his six potential pigeons were finishing their coffee. "When did they meet?"

"Recently, I think. Ryan's been in the jungles mostly."

"Now he's vanished? With Luz Cebellos and the Kern boy?"

"We'll find them," I said. "And there's one more—Bill Kern. He's been in the middle of it from the start, and he's missing again, too. I think he's doing more than gamble the money away, could have been doing more all along."

"Bill Kern?" Dutch said. "Yes. Perhaps you're right."

He stood up. The six gamblers were paying their check, leaving the table. Dutch laid his money on the bar.

"How have the games been going?" I said.

"Fine. The games are always fine." He watched the six men leaving. For a moment he seemed to stare at his own image in the long bar mirror. Tall and dignified. "It's odd, but I used to think there was nothing more important than a good poker game. Winning, moving on to the next game."

He smiled at me, and followed the others out.

◼ ◼ ◼

Even the rain is harsher in Jamaica. Colder and wetter, seeping into the crumbling houses. I parked two blocks from Luz Cebellos's house, and walked. I walked warily, alert. Extremes are explosive in the Jamaicas of the world. Heat, or cold, or rain.

I passed a store-front church. Singing flowed out into the rain. Vigorous singing, loud and fervent. Full and rich, strong and yet humble. A hundred voices packed into a narrow room side by side, singing their power in another world and their hope in this one. Strong and dignified and together, like the early Christians in Rome whose belief made them at once the equal of Caesar.

The comfortable wonder what *they* want, the people of the dark streets and leaking slums. The comfortable want to help, many of them, want to give a share of the warmth. If only *they* will cooperate, be reasonable. Rome wasn't built in a day. But the comfortable don't walk these streets, see the eyes in the doorways full of fear and hate. The eyes that watched me pass, didn't know me, but would kill me with the rage of impotence.

What they want, the dispossesed, is all. All and now. Denied by too many for too long to deny themselves. They want Rome now. The weak and the shallow want it for themselves, the strong and the full want it for all.

The rain fell steadily, the singing faded behind, and there was light in an upstairs room of Luz Cebellos's house. I listened at the door. Far off there was movement. Closer, there was another sound. Like an animal breathing in the night.

I tried the door. It was unlocked. My gun out, I stepped into darkness. Only the sibilant breathing like the beat of a pulse somewhere ahead. I inched forward, sliding my feet in the dark hall the way a blind man walks an unfamiliar street.

He lay at the foot of the stairs. Unconscious, and his face emerged as my eyes adjusted—the skinny Latin dandy with the powerful arms. Drunk? Drugs? I bent, smelled the whisky, and saw the shine of blood. In his hair, a wound.

I sensed the tiger.

Another breathing. A presence. Somewhere back beyond the stairs. Filling the darkness all around me. A tiger in the jungle, motionless and everywhere. Slowly, I moved back toward it, feeling it grow larger and expand from wall to wall. The glint of metal. A low voice.

"He was there when I came in. Who is he?"

Tom Craig stepped out of the deeper dark under the stairs. He lowered a small gun, looked toward the fallen dandy.

"Luz's lover, stud, I'm not sure what," I said. "What are you doing here?"

"We went to see Sam Tower. Away for the weekend, according to his wife. Town business." A soft whisper. "We can't find one truck driver, Wallace is tracing him. It's not a job for two, so I tried to think of where Bradley or Ryan might go, and I remembered the address Luz had given us. It occurred to me that Luz and Ryan could have known each other before, might hide at her place, so I came. I found him on the floor, searched him to find out who he was, and then heard you."

"You saw no one else?"

"No." He looked upward. "But someone is up there."

"Let's see," I said.

We went up. The light was in the front bedroom. The door was closed. Craig kicked it open, I went in.

Luz paced alone. A bottle and two glasses stood on a table. She whirled, alarmed, and then changed to anger.

"Where the hell have you two been? When do I get paid?"

"Ryan paid you," Craig said coldly. "Don't try—"

"He did not! I want—"

I said, "What happened down there? From the top."

"Happened?" She looked surprised. "It all went perfectly. We surprised the guards, freed the Kern boy and maybe ten other Americans, locked up the guards, and walked out. We got the Kern boy into the car, the others ran for the river, and we drove right back over the bridge. We—"

"The bridge?" I said.

"That wasn't the plan!" Craig snapped.

"Don't tell me, I didn't know any plan. Ask Ryan."

"Go on," I said.

"We went to a different motel in Eagle Pass to wait for you two. When you didn't appear, Ryan said you must have gone straight to the second rendezvous. He said something might have gone wrong, decided we had better split up. Ryan paid off the Mexican, headed off with Kern to meet you, and I got a plane in San Antonio and came home. I've been waiting ever since."

Craig said, "You're lying."

"Lying?" Her Indian face was cold. "I want my money."

"Bradley called," Craig said. "He said that you and Ryan were both with him."

"Called? When?"

I told her.

"Early?" She nodded. "We got gas and rented a car for me. After that we split."

Craig laughed.

"There was another call," I said. "To the Mexican police telling them where Craig and I were waiting for you all."

"Not me! How would I have known where you were?"

Craig stepped to her. He hit her full in the face with his fist. She went down flat on her back, skirt up over her hips, blood trickling from her mouth. She crawled to her knees, got up, and tried to hit Craig. He punched her again, hard. She slammed against the wall, came off clawing, and he knocked her down in a heap.

She lay on the floor. Craig stood over her neither angry nor vicious. Cool and methodical, force without emotion.

"You bastard," she said, and got up again.

She had a knife. From somewhere under her dress. She held it low and forward. Craig took the knife and knocked her down again. Simple power, the stronger.

"You knew where we were," Craig said.

She brushed her black hair from her dark face, licked her blood.

"All right, I knew you were in Mexico. But Ryan said the plan was changed, we went straight back to Eagle Pass. The rest was what I told you, and I made no phone calls. You can believe it, or go to hell."

"What happened to Bill Kern?" I said.

"I never saw him after we got to Eagle Pass."

Craig said, "Did Ryan or Brad talk about going anywhere?"

"Just the second hideout. You owe me money."

"You'll get it," Craig said coldly.

I said, "Did Ryan say anything about anyone else? Someone he worked for or with? Did Brad Kern?"

She shook her head.

"When did Nestor meet Ryan?" I said. "How?"

"I don't know. I only saw them together those few times."

"After they went to work for Wallace Kern?"

Craig pointed to the bottle and glasses. "Who's been here with you?"

"Not Ryan or the Kern boy."

"The man who was with you earlier?" I said.

She was up now, brushing her skirt. "Why?"

"Because he's down in the hall. Unconscious."

She went out the door first. When we caught up with her she was bending over the man. She stood up.

"You saw no one?" Craig said. "Heard nothing?"

"No," she said. "He only left twenty minutes or half an hour ago. I was sick of him."

We left her standing over the unconscious Latin. She would get him help. Out in the rain of the grimy street, we stood in the shadows. Craig had parked in the opposite direction.

"You think it was Ryan?" Craig said.

"Whoever," I said, "he must have come for Luz, and been scared off by you."

"There was no change of plan, Dan. Ryan lied to her."

"Or someone lied to him. Someone he would believe."

"Like Bradley? Or Bill? One of the family?"

"Unless Luz is lying," I said. "If it was all Ryan, I wonder if he knows Fred Sarguis."

"I better find out. Or find Ryan."

"You do that. I'll try for Bill Kern. Back where I began."

"Except the game may be different now," Craig said.

24

Long past seven o'clock, the rain stopped in New Canaan, but the small house was still dark. Near midnight. I parked up the street. No one answered the door. I used my keys.

The small, shabby rooms were still empty. I stood in the bedroom. Where had Laura gone? Did I want to know?

I left the bedroom. In the living room I lay down on the couch. Except for the morning in the motel in Eagle Pass, and a few hours on the planes, I hadn't slept since Wednesday night in this house, and it could be a long wait.

* * *

The hands touched me. Warmth flowed over me soft and heavy. I wanted to curl up in the warmth, burrow down. Float away. Not open my eyes, come back to the cold. But I opened them.

She was bent over me, her breasts loose under her shirt close to my face, her hands busy with a blanket. She was tucking me in, covering me on the couch.

"Where were you?" I said.

She went on tucking. "Go back to sleep."

"Not now." I sat up. "Tell me."

She let the blanket drop, went across the dark room and sat in an armchair. I switched on a lamp. She looked at the lamp as if she wasn't sure she had ever seen it before.

"Wallace dropped by earlier today, and he told me where you had all gone and why. Bill hadn't told me. He wasn't off on a binge, gambling and writing bad checks. He had gone somewhere for a good reason, and he hadn't told me anything about it. He came home and didn't talk to me, went away again and didn't tell me where or why."

She sat tall in the chair. I remembered the long curve of her body, the wide warmth of her hips.

"There could be a reason," I said.

"A reason I don't know," she said. "Perhaps a reason I've never really known. And that's where I went, Dan. I wanted to see where he had been going all these years, at least some of it. I wanted to see her."

"Connie Hall?"

"You told me her name, I found her address in the phone book. She wasn't home. I walked a long time in the Village, went to some of those taverns he had talked about. I even went to see the father of that girl who was killed. Stahl. He wasn't at his hotel. So I came home." She leaned her head back, closed her eyes. Her long legs were stretched out in wet black slacks. "Perhaps it was us. Why I had to look."

With the rain stopped the small room was cold, the temperature falling toward December. She shivered.

"All the years he had run with his demons toward an illusion. Pushed by an irrational force, and I understood when he couldn't take me along even in his mind. This time the force is rational, there should be a place for me." Her eyes opened. "Have I been wrong all these years? A fool? Was I ever really part of him, or was I the one chasing an illusion? His demons not his excuse, but mine?"

"If you want an answer, I can't give it to you," I said. "I only know what I want, not what you want. I hope I do."

"Must I let him go, Dan?"

"Can you let him go?"

A small town, even near a city, has a silence the city never knows. Seasons have meaning. There is time and place.

"I think I already have. Perhaps even before last Wednesday night. When you sent him home and he wasn't the same. I think it was I who wasn't the same." She moved in the chair as if her bones hurt, unable to get comfortable. "Objective, that's how I felt tonight on the Village streets. The people were strangers, and he was one of them. Thinking about him, sad, but no longer able to help him. Thinking about myself."

She thought about herself. "I wondered if it hadn't all been my fault, in a way. By holding onto him, being the noble wife, the loyal martyr. Perhaps all he ever wanted was the right to be irresponsible, and all I gave him was guilt. I held him, when what he wanted was to be let go. My loyalty only another demon. Thinking of him was my illusion. Perhaps the best gift I can give him is to think of myself."

The stump of my lost arm was aching. The rain and cold, and a tension. I hadn't really wanted a woman since Marty. I wanted this one. With me. But what did she want? I got up.

"I can't tell you that, Laura," I said, walked around in the shabby room. "I can tell you that Bill could have some more reasons for running this time." I told her everything that had happened since our Wednesday night, here and in Mexico. "He's been in the center of it from the start. He has money. He's gambling, but not only that the way he did in the past. He leaves the table. He's the only one who seems to have known everyone *before* Brad Kern was jailed. For all we know he could be the man behind the whole scheme."

"Selling a defective batch of medicine? Oh, no, Dan."

"He'd do anything for money. He's close to Brad. He has access to Kern Labs and the antibiotics. He brought Ryan and Cebellos to Wallace Kern. He was the contact with Cebellos the night Cebellos died. Think, Laura. For yourself. Objective."

The struggle inside her was physical, visible. A shivering, and not from the cold now. Her lips moving, working.

"He . . . he . . . *was* different." She closed her fist, hammered her thigh. "No. He was . . . detached. He was . . . When he came home he was . . . preoccupied. Yes. Preoccupied. Almost . . . knowing—"

It was a struggle for her. She had thought about Bill in one way for so long. To think about him in another way was hard. An observer seeing him clear.

"*Knowing?*" She said the word the way someone would who is trying to remember if she had heard it before. "He acted as if he knew something. 'A man has to know things.' He said that."

I heard an echo. Of what? From where?

"Does Bill know Fred Sarguis?" I said. "A competitor."

"Yes, but that was a long time ago, Dan. Almost a year, and it was Sarguis who approached him."

"Approached him about what?"

"Information about Kern Labs. To sell secret data. Bill didn't do it. He had no information about Kern Labs to sell."

"No," I said. "But Bill would take money and not deliver. That's his pattern. And maybe he finally had to deliver."

In the chair she clasped her knees, rocked.

"He *couldn't* have done anything, Dan. It's not in him. He's a gentle man who never got what he wanted, never found what he did want. He married me when he never should have. His father opposed the marriage. It was the last straw. The final break with his father. We never had children. I couldn't—"

"Laura?" I said. "Let him go."

She stopped rocking.

"For me," I said.

She sat there looking around the small, plain room almost like a stranger. Then she smiled and got up. She kissed me. We went into the bedroom. It told me something, and I wanted it, but I wasn't sure it told me all that I wanted to know.

* * *

Laura held the phone out. "He wants to talk to you. Wallace."

A clear morning sun in the bedroom, the sharp chill of a day that was suddenly winter.

"Me? How—?"

"I told him."

What I wanted to know? I took the receiver.

"Sam Tower is still away, but Craig and I found the last driver," Wallace Kern said. He made no comment on where I was. He had his own problem. "They all deny diverting any rejected batch, insist they took all of them to the dump."

"Then—?"

He stopped me. "But three times recently batches of the same antibiotic were handled oddly. By three different drivers."

"Oddly how?"

"They were held late at the loading dock, not released and trucked until past four P.M. The drivers work until four-thirty, and the dump closes down at the same time. Union rules."

"The batches were at the dump overnight? Unburned?"

"The trucks left loaded, the dump closed up. In the morning the drivers unloaded, and the batches were burned."

"But maybe not the same batches," I said. "What was wrong with the three batches?"

"Two were below standard, one was contaminated. All would seem normal to a doctor or pharmacist in the field, and they wouldn't have been as deadly as those Mexican reports indicated they were."

"You're saying they were cut later, adulterated?"

His silence at the other end of the line was my answer. I watched a bird on a bare tree outside Laura's window.

"Why were the batches handled differently?"

"Memo's from our production supervisor: Hold until four P.M. He says he never sent any memos, and Craig and I agree that the signatures look like forgeries."

"Who could send memos like that?"

"All our executives have the memo forms, from myself on down. Anyone who knew our offices could get forms, for that matter."

"It's Sunday," I said. "Where does Fred Sarguis live?"

"If I know him, he'll be at his offices."

On a winter Sunday morning the downtown business streets of New York are almost clear. In a cloudless sky the tall glass and steel building where Caldwell Pharmaceutical had its offices thrust upward like a knife, a glittering rocket eager for outer space.

Wallace Kern and his Cadillac were already there, the only car parked in the long canyon of buildings. The weekend guard stopped us in the marble lobby. Mr. Sarguis had signed in. A call got us invited up, and on the twenty-third floor the maroon carpet stretched behind the double glass doors like a grass field on some alien planet.

Sarguis himself greeted us at the portal to his imperial corner office. His smile was sardonic.

"What an honor, Wallace! Sunday, too. The yacht, it is sunk? The golf course is closed?"

If Sarguis had more than one suit they were all the same color and style, and all in the same rumpled condition.

"Five days doesn't give you time to outscheme everyone, Fred?" Wallace Kern said.

"Opportunity knocks every day, eh?" Sarguis grinned.

He led us into his office, waved us to seats. He had barely glanced at me, but he'd seen me and knew me. The cloudless sky beyond the high windows gave me vertigo, on the edge of a vast precipice. At his desk, Sarguis sat back and waited. I told him about the antibiotics. About the sale in Mexico, and the possible source in the bad batches at Kern Labs.

"So that is what has been happening, eh?" Sarguis said, shook his head. "A neat scheme, profitable, but adulterated? Not good for business. A little dumping of our excess production on the illegal market, that is common enough, eh, and lucrative, but it's not like you to sell bad stuff, Wallace. Your sales are looking good, a nice balance sheet."

On his feet Wallace Kern's boyish face was red and angry. "If anyone sold defective drugs, Sarguis, it would be you! You'd sell poison to make a dime profit! You've been meeting in secret with my assistant Sam Tower. What have you—?"

Sarguis eyed me. "Fortune has imagination, or a reason to lie. I don't know what either of you is talking about."

"How do you know Kern's sales look good?" I said.

Sarguis's eyes glittered, but he said nothing.

"You approached Bill Kern for inside information about Kern Labs. Bill would do a lot for money, but he didn't have anything to deliver, did he? So you turned to Sam Tower. Bill probably took your money, and that gave you a hold on him. With Tower and Bill you could get almost anything from Kern Labs."

"I have lawyers, Fortune. I think—"

The telephone interrupted him. He listened, held the receiver out to Wallace Kern. "For you."

Wallace Kern took the phone. "When?"

He listened, and then put the phone down.

"Tom Craig," he said. He sat down. "They found Bradley. In Texas. In a grave. Murdered."

* * *

Dark outside the Centre Street windows, and it was no longer Captain Gazzo's office. The shades were up, the desk clear and clean, the lights bright, and I had filled Captain Pearce in on everything that had happened.

"They found the grave at that farmhouse near Rocksprings," Pearce said. "He must have gone there, or been taken, after you went through. No identification, but they knew about the jailbreak, recognized him. Shot in the head with a rifle. Some food in the house had been eaten, a bed slept in. One bed." He was as clean and crisp as the shiny office. "You think this Joe Ryan is connected to those Bolivian gunmen? They did kill Cebellos and the girl? We can close it?"

I shook my head. "Brad Kern wasn't in it alone, I'm sure of that, and I don't think Ryan's the end of the chain. Someone used Brad Kern. We're tracing the antibiotics."

"Damn," Pearce said. "But we have to be sure. No one can get away with killing a policeman, even inadvertently."

I looked around at the shiny office. "Gazzo once said he didn't see why killing a cop was worse than killing anyone else. Maybe it wasn't as bad. Part of a cop's job. His risk."

Pearce nodded. "He might have been right, but it's a matter of social order, Fortune. We're the law, the power, and we have to be respected. They have to know they can't defy the power."

"Power at the center of everything, Captain?"

"It always is," he said.

25

The funeral was on Thursday. December now.

Since Monday I'd beaten the bushes of Manhattan's gambling action for any sign or word of Bill Kern. The police had a bulletin out coast to coast for Joe Ryan. The Texas police were trying to pick up a trail for either of them.

No results yet, and the family stayed close to home, waiting for the body and the funeral.

A small cortège from church to grave. Only family.

They buried Bradley Kern in a graveyard a few miles from the plant and the big Connecticut house. An old graveyard choked with bramble vines and winter grass, fallen stones under the trees on the gray December day. Eroded old headstones with names like Putnam, and Stark, and Kern. Josiah Kern, Israel Kern, Col. Obadiah Higgins Kern, and, in the shadow of the imposing monument of the late W. Jason Kern, founder of Kern Laboratories, Inc., now Bradley Kern.

Episcopal robes blowing in the wind, the austere minister read the service and the eulogy.

" . . . *a young man, taken from us . . .*"

Slim in veiled black, Marjorie Kern talked to the fresh earth of the waiting grave.

'. . . that awful country. Why? Oh, Bradley. I tried to show you. I did. Why didn't you listen to me? What can I do now? What will I do? Why didn't you think of . . ."

She leaned on Dr. Tom Craig. Clung to him. Veil blowing, her head rested on his shoulder. Craig supported her, firm and clear-eyed, looking straight ahead at the minister.

　　　 ▦　▦　▦

". . . *the Lord giveth, and the Lord taketh away* . . . "

Neither firm nor clear-eyed, Wallace Kern looked straight at nothing, supported not even himself. His heavy shoulders sagged like a stuffed bear gone too soft, and in his swollen boyish face the pale blue eyes moved right and left, around and around, as if searching for something.

Anna Botha stood with him. Stiff in her black, the brown, beauty-contest face set not in sorrow but in anger. Her eyes looked straight at the coffin, unwavering. Only her hands moved, gentle on Wallace Kern's arm, comforting.

　　　 ▦　▦　▦

I stood with Laura. I listened to the minister, and to the ceaseless mumble of Marjorie Kern behind the minister and the wind. I looked at Marjorie Kern and Craig, at Wallace Kern and Anna Botha.

New partners. Openly now. A rearrangement of lives. A beginning at an ending.

　　　 ▦　▦　▦

Luz Cebellos stood apart. Alone. An uninvited surprise that no one had mentioned.

Sam Tower with his wife a few steps behind Wallace Kern.

Laura beside me.

"He should be here," she said. "Bill. At least that."

"If he knows," I said. "If he cares."

"Not for me," she said. "He loved Bradley. As much as he could anyone. Dan, he would be here if he could. I know that."

"They're looking for him."

"Dan," she said, "I'm afraid. For him."

"*. . . to the earth . . .*"

Slowly lowering.

■ ■ ■

The sound of shovels. Cars starting in the December wind.

"You know how sorry I am, Wallace," Sam Tower said.

"What did you sell Fred Sarguis?" Wallace Kern said. "How much did he pay you?"

Thin and gaunt, Tower was gray in his carefully mended black suit. His Yankee face like granite.

"I sold Sarguis nothing."

"Rejected antibiotics? Black-market profits?"

"You accuse *me* of—!"

Anna Botha said, "Weren't you safe enough with Bradley in a Mexican jail?"

Tower turned sharply to his wife, "Wait in the car." He turned back to Wallace Kern, pointed at Anna Botha. "Bradley listened to her radical poison. Are you going to listen to her now? Is she going to become a vice-president too? Young enough to be your daughter? Someone else to destroy Kern Labs!"

"Why were you meeting Sarguis?" Wallace Kern said.

"Business! Something you know little about, and what you do know I taught you! *I've* built Kern Labs, kept it going!"

A slow astonishment crossed Wallace Kern's puffy face. He looked back toward the silent new grave, and then at Tower.

173

"Without you I couldn't have started to run the company. I've said how grateful I am for that."

"Grateful?" Tower spat the word. "Old Sam, the faithful dog. Special assistant. I should have been president. Not even a vice-president. Tom Craig, men I hired for your father, outsiders, they're vice-presidents. Well, Fred Sarguis knows my value. He'll give me the position I deserve."

I said, "Your value to Sarguis is what you know about Kern."

"My value is my ability! I know how to protect a company, keep it alive. Without me, this company will die."

"Survive just to survive?" Anna Botha said. "A company has to have some purpose that is more than just continuance. A company, and a nation. A person has to. There has to be right and wrong. More than just right for *me*, for the company, for the nation. There must be some things we can't do even to survive, Mr. Tower. There has to be a *right* bigger than survival. If there isn't, we're all no more than a condemned man proud of his large cell."

"You keep your crazy ideas away from me." Tower glared at her. "We've let your kind go too far. You probably put Bradley up to what he did. Money for your 'ideas'!"

"My kind?" Anna said. "A mulatto? A woman?"

"You can clear your desk," Wallace Kern said. "Tomorrow. You're fired, Sam."

The gaunt old man licked his thin lips in the wind of the graveyard. In the distance his wife waited at their car.

"Very well. I'll have a good job with Sarguis, get what I should have. I'll go, and I'll take what I know with me."

"Is that all you'll take?" I said. "You didn't go to Sarguis just recently the way you told me. You went to him a long time ago. But you stayed at Kern Labs. Maybe to be sure you were safe? You felt cheated at Kern. Maybe you wanted a little nest egg to take with you, so took those antibiotics and sold them."

"That, Fortune, is slander. Unless you have some proof, which you do not, and cannot."

He walked away. I saw his wife smile, speak to him. Then she stopped smiling, and looked past him to where we stood with the new grave behind us.

⬚ ⬚ ⬚

At the door of the small New Canaan house, Laura looked back.

"You think you have time?"

"Always," I said.

I followed her into the low living room.

"Dan!"

The room was a wreck. A hard and violent search. I went through the other rooms. They had all been searched.

"Who?" Laura said. "Why, Dan?"

I looked around at the mess.

"Did Bill leave anything in the house? Something someone would want? Valuable? Anything unusual?"

"Not that I know, Dan, and it's a small house."

"Could anything in the house help to locate him?"

"If there had been, I'd have located him."

I walked around among the open drawers and fallen chairs.

"Laura, it's possible that Bill is behind the drug scheme. He had the opportunity and the knowledge to a point, and he disappeared down in Texas, too."

"No, Dan, it's not possible."

"Then there's another possibility. We know five people who could have known everything from the start: Bradley himself, Nestor Cebellos, Adelita, Ryan, and Bill. Three of them are dead. Except for Ryan, and maybe one more person if Bill didn't plan it, Bill is the last one alive who might know why and who."

"If he knew, why didn't he tell? At least Wallace."

"Money, maybe, or because he thought he was helping Bradley, or because he did start it but now someone wants him gone."

"You think Ryan is looking for Bill." She sat down. "It had to catch up to him someday, didn't it? The gambling. Someday it had to get him into real danger."

"At least we know he's still loose," I said. "You're sure no one could have found any lead to him here?"

"What, Dan? I don't know where he is. I don't know anyone who does. There's nothing here—"

She sat there very quiet for a moment. Then she got up and went to the telephone table. The phone and the table lay on the floor, papers scattered around. Laura got down and pawed among the papers. Slowly, and then faster, and then stopped.

"I wrote it down," she said, "then didn't take it with me. Connie Hall's name and address. It's not here."

If Ryan, or whoever had searched, took the name and address, he had a reason to know who Connie Hall was.

■ ■ ■

The black door at 519 Hudson Street swung broken on its hinges. I got out my pistol, went in. The one-room jungle of plants, and photographs, and divided little areas packed with furniture was undisturbed, untouched.

Connie Hall sat in the tiny living room area as untouched as the room. In the same loose black dress and high heels that slimmed her legs and hid her shapeless figure. Her puffy face was blank. She didn't look at me.

"Where's Bill Kern," I said. "Do you know?"

"He kicked in the door," she said. "This apartment is all I have. He would have hurt me!"

"You told him where Bill is?"

"Why shouldn't I? What do I owe him? He comes here when he's broke, beaten, on the run. He goes home to her."

"Who was he? The man who kicked in the door?"

"I never saw him before. Big, an animal. Boots, a gun, a uniform. He would have hit—"

"What did you tell him?"

"Bill left three thousand dollars. He didn't want to take it to Mexico. Last Friday he called and told me to send a thousand to general delivery, El Paso, Texas."

Friday? Before the jailbreak?

"Sunday he sent a telegram, wanted a thousand in Phoenix, Arizona. Tuesday I sent the last to Kingman, Arizona."

"How long since the big man was here?"

"I don't know. An hour. He was going to hurt me. I won't be hurt. I couldn't let him ruin my face. I'm expecting a very good offer any day. You can see all that I've done."

She waved toward the playbills and photos that covered her walls. I stared at them, the mementoes that were more important than a man's life. I stepped closer to them. All the playbills with her name in the cast were the same three repeated over and over. The photos of players on stages were the same people on the same three stages. All the signed portraits of famous actors and actresses were signed in the same handwriting.

The whole apartment, with its polished brass and tiny imitation of elegance, was an illusion and a fantasy. An illusion of elegance, a fantasy of memory. No more real than the fantasy of her tragic romance with Bill Kern.

On Hudson Street I looked for a taxi. Ryan was after him, but for what reason? Bill Kern didn't look like a man fleeing from danger, and I didn't need a map to see in what direction he was going, or a crystal ball to guess the next stop.

26

When I landed it was afternoon in Las Vegas. When I found him it was long past dark.

A cold wind blew along the broad boulevard of the Strip where the revolving, blinking lights of the hotels enticed the tourists with perpetual holiday, the night women worked their trade on foot and from cars, and the gamblers, coatless and hands in pockets, shuffled from hotel to hotel in perpetual search for the place they knew waited somewhere with their big streak of luck. Bill Kern wasn't on the Strip.

A motel on the outskirts of downtown, with a dim cocktail lounge and a dingy casino. He was at the poker table. I stood behind him. He didn't notice me. He sat as stiffly as a condemned man in a cell who knows there is no hope for him, but who will go on until the end pretending there is, making the motions of someone who still expects to win it all.

I watched him not raise a flush against a nervous three jacks that had obviously failed to fill, and then call an obvious full house with three nines. It tapped him out, and he got up to go to the chip window. He saw me, nearly stumbled, then went on and laid five hundred dollars out for the chips.

"It won't help," I said.

"The lucky five," he said. "My comeback."

"First we talk," I said.

The dark lounge was half empty. Some middle-aged men and women sat at the bar with the look of people who sat on the same stools every night, lived in the lounge. A few couples shared tables, a man read a newspaper alone in one of the three booths, a youth commuted between another booth and the juke box. None of them wore boots or parts of uniforms. The middle booth was empty. We took it.

"Some way to hide," I said. "You might as well advertise."

"Where would I go, Fortune? The gambling rabbit," he said. "Who this time? Laura? My good brother again?"

He refused a drink. I had a beer. He acted as if nothing were different, nothing was new. Had he really left Eagle Pass before the jailbreak and didn't know? Or did he know too much, more than I did? From the start. Covering himself.

"I'm on my own this time," I said. "It's not about your gambling this time."

"What is it about? Laura?" A faint smile.

"Antibiotics," I said. "You know about the antibiotics?"

He sat there a moment. Then he nodded.

"Yes," he said, "and if you know, they must have gotten Bradley out. I'm glad."

"How much do you know about them? The antibiotics?"

His eyes flickered around the dark lounge, toward the noise of the poker table. "Fortune, I'm not important to you, or to anyone. Can't you just go back to Laura, or Wallace, and say you couldn't find me? Walk away? Leave me alone?"

"The antibiotics," I said. "The deal."

He shrugged. "Brad was taking them down to Mexico to help some South Americans who needed them."

"Who else knew? Your brother? Tom Craig?"

"I think so, but we never talked about it. They were insisting that Brad hadn't done anything, so wanted it quiet, I suppose. I really don't know."

"Marjorie and Anna Botha?"

"I said I don't really know."

"Sam Tower?"

"I've told you what I know."

"How much money did you take from Fred Sarguis? What did you have to deliver? When you took his money, or later."

He moved restlessly, and his hands twisted together on the booth table. He watched the hands, studied them.

"I had nothing I could deliver. I'll pay him back. He's high on my list of obligations."

"You knew the antibiotics were stolen from Kern Labs?"

He had been listening to the chips clicking at the poker table, his head half turned. Now he looked back at me.

"Rejected batches," I said. "Defective. Deadly."

"Defective?"

Startled. Some kind of shock. Or fear.

"Stolen from Kern Labs, taken to Mexico by Bradley, and sold for a nice profit," I said. "You'd do almost anything for money. You know about drugs. You have access to the plant. You knew Cebellos and his Mexican contacts. Motive and opportunity."

"Me?" The juke box blared out in a loud rock number. "The need and the opportunity. But that kind of thing takes more than that. Two other attributes I don't have, Fortune—the courage, and the desire."

All at once I believed him. He was right, and I believed the way he had said it. It wasn't in him, and he knew it. He knew it, and I knew it. The boldness and the desire to act.

"When did you leave Texas?" I said.

"On Friday."

"Before or after the jailbreak?"

"The moment Craig sent me back up to wait at the rendezvous. I just drove right on past to San Antonio. I wasn't really needed, no one would steal the food, and there was a game I'd heard about—" He shrugged.

"Someone made a telephone call that night to the Mexican police. Telling them where Craig and I were waiting for Ryan, Luz and Bradley."

"Not me. I was chasing aces in San Antonio. I didn't know where you were waiting anyway. No one told me."

He had left Eagle Pass before the jailbreak. He knew nothing that had happened at Eagle Pass, or after, because he had run away to gamble once more. No more than that. His weakness—and it had probably saved his life.

"Defective?" he said. "How could Brad be part of that? Are you sure, Fortune?"

"That's why those Bolivians were after Bradley, and anyone involved with him. We think he was fooled somehow, used."

He looked away toward the sounds of the poker game beyond the wall of the lounge, but I had seen the quick gleam in his eyes. The reflection of a thought. Almost eager.

"You know who used Brad, don't you," I said. "You knew all along, or you guessed later. That's how you've been getting some money. Not a lot, it wasn't anything big. Just a mistake that got Brad into trouble. But you've just realized how big it really is, figure you can get a lot more money."

"I know nothing more than I said."

"He won't pay you, Kern," I said. "Not with money. Brad Kern was murdered down there in Texas."

"Bradley!"

"Ryan broke him out, but they never met Craig and me. They didn't go to the rendezvous where you were supposed to be. They got rid of Luz Cebellos, and vanished. Brad was found dead at the rendezvous after Craig and I had gone home. Ryan must have taken him there, and killed him."

His teeth made a grating sound in the dim booth.

"Cebellos, Adelita, Bradley. Who's left?" I stood up. "We're going back to New York. You saved your life in Texas by taking off, but Ryan's looking for you, and he can follow a trail as well as I can. Wherever you're staying, we won't go back. If you brought anything with you, leave it. The next plane out isn't too soon."

When we left the lounge, Bill Kern looked toward the poker table. If I hadn't been there he would have stayed. One more hand. I pushed him toward the door, and he resisted even now.

"Ryan wouldn't have killed Cebellos."

"Such good friends?"

Out in the street I looked for a taxi.

"No, but Cebellos was important to get Bradley out of that jail. Ryan wouldn't have wanted—"

"Was Adelita important?"

The wind scoured the dark edge of the city. I half dragged him toward the brighter streets.

"I think they thought she had killed Cebellos," he said. "They never really had wanted her—"

The next plane out wasn't going to be soon enough.

He came out of the night near the motel behind us. Not twenty yards away. Alone in his boots, field jacket, and red beret. His automatic rifle raising toward us. I saw in his flat blank eyes that he was surprised to see me. I saw, too, that it wouldn't help me. One or two made no difference to Joe Ryan.

I pushed Bill Kern, dove for the street.

The single burst sprawled Bill Kern bleeding on the ground. A blow picked me up, flung me backwards on my feet.

Ryan fell on his face, the rifle flying away and clattering in the night.

Dutch Stahl had come out of the motel. He shot Ryan twice more on the ground.

The bullet had hit the heavy cloth of my pinned-up sleeve. I wasn't touched. Bill Kern lay unconscious, I couldn't tell where he was hit. He was breathing.

Ryan was dead. His face was almost peaceful.

I took the pistol from Stahl. A small .32-caliber revolver, short-barreled and chrome-plated. A woman's gun, and I knew at once—it was the gun that had shot Nestor Cebellos.

Stahl saw my face. "Kern guessed right. Ryan didn't kill Cebellos. Kern guessed a long time ago. He didn't care as long as I let him win some hands. I'd kill Nestor again."

"In the lounge," I said. "The man behind the newspaper. I only looked for boots, a uniform."

"I've been watching Kern. I know every dealer in Vegas, it wasn't hard to find him." He looked down at Ryan. "Nestor would never have taken Addie to Mexico. A new life. All in her mind, her fantasy. He never gave her a moment of happiness. Trouble, and misery, and pain. He lied to her, cheated her, used her, dragged her into the gutter, and threw her away. She let him. She always would. Until, one way or another, he destroyed her. I wasn't going to let him do it again, drag her into another dirty scheme. He'd never done an honest day's work, he never would. When she told me he was going to marry her again, give her a fine new life in Mexico, it was the last straw. I couldn't let him hurt her this time. So I shot him. I'd do it again. A hundred times."

A single man had come out of the motel, and gone back in. Faces stared from windows, but no one else came out. Dutch Stahl stood in the night as erect as ever, dignified in a dark blue suit. But his hair was ragged, and his fine old face had aged, loose and fallen. He brushed at his pale eyes.

"I'm glad I killed Nestor, only I wish I hadn't. If I hadn't, perhaps Addie would still be alive. My way of life killed her, didn't it? My world. The Cebelloses, the Bill Kerns, the Ryans, the Arizona Dutch Stahls."

Sirens had started in the distance. Coming closer. From two directions. A few more daring people, hearing the sirens, began to venture out. Staring, enjoying the violence.

"Fortune?" Stahl said. "Don't turn me in yet. Ryan wasn't alone. You said it. Nestor didn't bring him into this. Nestor wasn't in New York for a year until two months ago. Let me—"

"No," I said. "I'll do it."

"You know?"

I kneeled in the street beside Bill Kern. He was moving. I shook him. I had to try.

"Bill? Did Ryan kill Adelita?"

His eyes opened slowly, all surface. " . . . think so . . . hotel where you . . . found me . . . not the . . . Latins . . . found me first . . . Laura . . . made me . . . made me . . ."

He passed out again, and the police were in the street. They took Bill Kern to the hospital, Ryan to the morgue, and Dutch Stahl to jail. They talked to me. I told them the whole story. I asked them to hold their report to New York and Connecticut for a few hours. I could get to New York before anyone knew what had happened out here. I could finish it before the last killer could get away.

27

I was wrong.

He was waiting in my apartment. Luz Cebellos was with him. The first wet snow fell outside my windows in the December dawn.

"You worked it out, Dan?" Dr. Tom Craig said.

"I worked it out," I said. "I should have sooner."

"You should have," Craig agreed.

He was sitting behind my desk. His gun lay on the desk. Luz Cebellos stood against the door. She had a gun too, her Indian face impassive with the heritage of thousands of years.

"The Las Vegas police reported?" I said. "They told you what happened?"

"I'm not an amateur, Dan. Ryan called in five times a day when he was on an operation, left a message. He didn't call at midnight. I started checking. Laura told me you had gone after Ryan. I called a friend in Vegas, got the story, and guessed what you were doing. My plans have been made for some time. If you didn't come here it would have been tighter, but now I'll get a good head start."

"Luz goes too? From the first?"

"Not before that day on the boat." He looked at the woman at the door. "But we've found we're two of a kind."

"The fight an act for me? You hit that boyfriend?"

"Mostly an act. She nearly made a mistake, so I hit her. I think we both got carried away. She handles a knife, doesn't she?" He smiled. "I didn't want the punk to see me."

"Marjorie Kern?"

He shrugged. He looked at his watch. "We've got some time. Tell me how you decided on me?"

He wasn't a man whose violence showed on the outside. I didn't fool myself. He'd killed, or had someone else kill, five people, not to mention the sick Bolivians, and he was in my office with a gun. If he wanted to talk, I'd talk.

"Someone used Brad Kern. Not Ryan alone, no connection to Kern Labs. Marjorie hasn't got the brains, and she'd get her money out of some man. Wallace wouldn't have used Brad that way. Tower had a motive, but Brad wouldn't have believed him. Fred Sarguis could find fifty easier ways, and Anna Botha wouldn't hurt rebels. Bill Kern doesn't have the guts. You were the only one who fitted."

"That's afterthought," he said. "Why think of me at all?"

"Dutch Stahl said it—Ryan wasn't Nestor Cebellos's kind of man, too violent. Ryan denied ever being in South America, and maybe he wasn't, but he was a Marine, and so were you."

He nodded. "I knew him in the Corps. He looked me up after he returned from Africa. Hard to think he's dead. The girl's father. You can't relax, get careless, no matter how simple a situation looks. He should have known better." He shook his head, a stupid mistake. "What else, Dan?"

"That anonymous phone tip to the Mexicans. You didn't tell me the plan until we were in Mexico. You didn't tell Bill Kern. You couldn't have told Bradley. Luz said she knew, but she didn't. That was the mistake she almost made when you hit her—she said she didn't know at first, because she didn't. So only Ryan knew where we were. He called the Mexicans. But why?"

"Tell me."

"Because you wanted me out of the way, and wanted to look out of it all yourself. The best alibi when Brad turned up dead. It looked like Ryan had changed the plan, but he hadn't. You were pretty confident that the Mexicans had no proof against us, that the break had succeeded. Because if Ryan had been caught, he would never have told where we were. The Mexicans had no reason to ask, no reason to suspect anyone else was part of the break and waiting in Mexico. So when the Mexican cops caught us you knew the escape had worked. It was proof that Ryan had made his call, had Bradley in the States. What happened wasn't a change of plan by Ryan, it was the plan. Your plan."

"Very good," Craig said.

"Then there was Adelita. Bill said it was the gunmen who knocked me out that night, but it was you and Ryan. Laura told you and Wallace that Bill was in a hotel. You found the hotel through Adelita because Dutch was there too, and got there first. You wanted to get rid of the gunmen. You had Bill say they had gone after Adelita, knowing I'd call the police. You got the gunmen there, probably by telling them to meet you on the roof if they wanted some information about Brad Kern."

"Right," Craig said. "Ryan was watching them."

"You poisoned Adelita, fired those shots on the roof. Or on another roof. I remember a shot seemed to come from the edge of the parapet. You didn't care if the gunmen were killed or taken, they'd be out of your way long enough. But they, or Ryan, shot Gazzo and the police gunned them down for you."

"From across the street. Ryan was a good shot. A policeman is easy to tell, any one of them would have done."

The epitaph for a good policeman? Any cop would have done. Gazzo's death only a tool for Tom Craig.

"How did you get Bill to play along?"

He rocked in my chair. "Said they were killers from Mexico after Brad and Adelita. If we told the police, we'd have to reveal that Brad had really taken drugs into Mexico no matter how good his intentions. I added some cash, pay for his help. Later I convinced him that we hadn't wanted it to happen that way, but they were killers anyway. I needed his help to free Brad, would pay him. It wasn't too hard."

"Why kill Adelita? There were other ways to get those gunmen."

"Ryan was sure she had shot Cebellos, and without Cebellos she was unreliable, dangerous. She knew just enough so that I didn't want her running loose. Since I had to stop those *pistoleros*, two birds looked like a good plan."

"Why not Bill Kern too? Why wait?"

"Useful, and no problem as long as he didn't know the truth about the drugs. Some cash kept his mind busy. Cebellos's murder had already caused too much furor. By the time Bill learned the truth, he could be handled along with Bradley."

"Only he ran off too soon. You might have guessed."

"Yes, my mistake."

"One you sent Ryan to correct in Vegas," I said. "Is it my turn now?"

He looked surprised. "You're no long-range danger to me. My connection to Ryan will come out from Marine records. Bill will tell the police about Adelita and the gunmen. The drug deal will be obvious. Besides, I like you, Dan. All I need is some time."

In the end we're all human. I wanted to believe him. Had to believe him. A killer, and a hero. Both at once, and somehow unaware of the difference. Could I believe him?

"You and Ryan hijacked the rejected batches? Told Bradley it was a mercy shipment? Sent him down to Mexico?"

"With Ryan along to handle the business end. Brad thought it was free." He smiled at Brad Kern's naivete. "We used false names so if Bradley hadn't been caught they could never have traced it to us. In jail the Mexicans got his real name. It was only a matter of time before the cat was out of the bag. We had to free him. Cebellos took too long setting it up. Then he was killed, and I had to scramble to try to cover up."

"The Bolivian Schweitzer," I said.

"Yes," he laughed. "That came in handy, made it easier to sell the stuff, and easier to use Bradley."

Another tool. There wasn't any difference or contradiction for him. Heroism doesn't necessarily make a man pure, anymore than martyrdom necessarily makes a man a saint.

"Why?" I said.

He swiveled in my chair. "I'm going back, Dan. Somewhere down there, I don't want to say where. I've done all I want to here. They're wonderful countries down there—wild, open, and they can be rich. I can do things there. The governments and rebels are all useless. They're ruining it, both sides. I can build a new force, a new nation."

He rocked, looked at his watch, restless in my chair. "But that takes money. I saw all those rejected batches going up in smoke, saw how easy it was to hijack them undetected. Too good an opportunity to miss, and it would have been fine if Bradley had been smarter, or that old man hadn't shot Cebellos and sent you and the police buzzing around. Even then I might have slipped through if Bill Kern hadn't gone gambling."

An opportunity. The funds for his plans. A challenge no different from bringing survivors out of a jungle, or building a hospital where it was needed. Businessman, and jungle doctor. Team player, and loner. Pragmatist, and dreamer. Hero, and nightrunner. Action and power above all. Achilles.

He stood up. "Time to go."

He had rope and handcuffs all ready. He cuffed and tied me on and to the bed, and gagged me tight.

"They'll come for you," he said.

If they didn't come for me in time, he couldn't help that. Luz went out first. She had said nothing at all, not needing words now. Craig stopped in the doorway, looked back.

"A naive boy, an old man trying to protect his daughter, and a failure running from himself. That's what beat me." He shook his head. "Unbelievable, and unpredictable." He grinned at me. "Then, that's what makes life interesting, isn't it?"

The door closed, and they were gone.

* * *

Captain Pearce found me late in the afternoon. I was still on the bed. Craig tied knots the way he did everything else.

"The Vegas cops reported you'd come back last night," Pearce explained. "When you didn't show up, or answer your phone, I had a hunch. Who was it? Where is he?"

I told him, shook my head. "You won't find him."

They didn't. Not a trace. Craig had had it all planned, all set up, and they never even smelled him.

Marjorie Kern took it badly. After some hysterics, she tried to battle Wallace's divorce action. She lost, but she came away with a good settlement, and soon married again. An older executive in a national beer company who lived in a big suburban house with a lawn. I understand Marjorie, what she needs and wants from men. I don't understand the men. What does she have to offer? What do they need that she gives them?

Sam Tower joined Fred Sarguis's firm. He lasted less than a year. When Sarguis had no more use for him, he had to go back to work as sales manager for a small drug company in Manhattan, commuting silently from Connecticut every day.

Nothing happened to Sarguis.

Wallace Kern and Anna Botha were married after his divorce came through. I was invited to the wedding.

"Building a business isn't a small achievement," Anna Botha said, smiled at Wallace. "Doing something with it is bigger. Something important, something worthwhile. There's a whole world that needs medicines."

I'm not sure that Wallace knew what she was talking about, or really cared. Bradley's death had brought them together, she's young and beautiful, and Wallace needed someone. But she'll make him move. His money and power, her brains and drive. They could make a hell of a team.

Dutch Stahl went to prison. He'll be a good prisoner in a minimum prison, and if he doesn't die there he'll be out in a few years. He'll go back to his cards and hotels. It won't be the same. There isn't a lot of difference between a cell and anonymous hotel rooms for an old man alone.

Bill Kern got out of the hospital and came home. He took a job with Wallace. Remorse for Bradley, I think. Laura left him, and moved in with me.

We wanted each other, and settled down nicely. She was what I'd been looking for since Marty. We had six months.

"He's gone again, Dan. Wallace called me."

"He'll come back."

"I know," she said.

When an animal is injured, or lost in a strange area, it adjusts or goes under. Some of the adjustments are remarkable. Man is the same. When we find ourselves in a situation we can neither live with nor change, we adjust. The adjustments we can make are amazing, too. The twisted paths we create to go on living. Like the timid man who wants so much to be strong and free that he never steps out his door, but lives locked in his room with cats and a TV for company. Odd, self-defeating, but the only way we can go on living.

"He won't change," I said. "The world won't change or get better, so he'll go on as always. His life won't get more worthwhile to him. His failure won't get less. His hunger won't go away, and his dreams aren't going to be found or forgotten. He'll try to accept, but the blank wall will come up, and he'll run again."

"I know," she said.

"And when he comes home," I said, "you'll be there."

"Dan?"

"Go ahead," I said. "It's where you have to be."

Her adjustment, and his. Their way of surviving. He can't tell her, or himself, that he doesn't really want her, and she can't let him destroy himself no matter how much he wants to.

*   *   *

A year later Captain Pearce got an advance copy of a Bolivian news release. With profound regret, the Bolivian Army reported the death of Dr. Tom Craig in a bloody attack they had made on the camp of a mercenary force of right-wing invaders. Unaware that Dr. Craig was even in Bolivia, the attack-force commander had not identified the body for some days, and had no explanation for the presence of the hero doctor with such criminals.

Pearce looked out his window at the busy city. "You know what I really feel bad about, Fortune? Those two gunmen we killed. They hadn't really done anything."

"Yeh," I said. "They got his fingerprints? Positive identification?"

"No," Pearce said. "I called. The body was too shot up and decomposed by the time it was identified to be brought out. But he was well-known down there, and the photo looks like him."

Out in the winter sun a long way from Bolivia, I walked to the subway. A gray photo of a shot-up body rotting in a jungle. Buried where it had fallen. No explanation of what he had been doing, and no mention of a woman with him.

It was one way Tom Craig could have ended, playing out his own daring game. It fitted, but Luz Cebellos should have been with him, and I wouldn't be surprised too much if, someday, somewhere, he turned up again. Him, or someone just like him.

No one ever found it easy to kill Achilles.

THE END

A Sneak Peek at the next Dan Fortune Mystery

**Read the first chapter
of the next exciting Dan Fortune mystery**

The Slasher
**by Dennis Lynds
#10 in the Edgar Award-winning Dan Fortune mystery series**

Each year we make it easier to do more faster with less time to think about what we do or why we do it. Maybe we want it that way. Or someone does.

I thought about it as I watched the remote towns in the snow outside the train windows, and I thought about Marty and her telephone call from nearly three thousand miles and almost five years away. I thought about how her voice across all those miles and years had sounded just as it had close to my ear in the small bedrooms of our good times together. I thought about her words, "It's my husband's niece, Dan. Someone killed her. I need your help."

As the train rattled along, I finished my fourth beer. I had forgotten how good it was to sit with a drink while looking out at places I seldom got to see. The mammoth Mississippi River was frozen from bank to bank. Then there was Dodge City, and now the austere high plains of Colorado under a vast winter sky. We were a long way from Eighth Avenue, New York, New York. In the morning, we would be in Los Angeles.

As the train swayed around the high curves of Raton Pass, I thought about Marty. Martine Adair, actress and once my woman. She left me to marry her director because she wanted permanence, wanted the rewards of here and now, wanted her existence testified to by the recognition of others. They were the needs of our time – needs a private detective with a one-room office/apartment could never fill.

Marty was the only woman I still saw in store windows, in the swing of a full skirt, in the vanishing heel of a boot. She was the woman I thought about late at night alone, the way I thought about my missing left arm. And she had called me, to investigate the death of her husband's niece.

But there were private detectives in California.

Maybe what she really wanted was to see me, I thought. To talk to me after five years, maybe even to? ...

I went for another beer. The train moved on across New Mexico through a sweeping land of desert and arid mountains white with winter snow.

We never give up, do we? Deep down we know it was all some kind of mistake that they left us. Was that the real reason I was on the train? I could have gotten on a jet in Chicago, or even a private charter in New York. But the longer I took to get to L.A., the longer it'd be before I had to meet Marty and find out what she really wanted from me.

I drank my beer and stared out at darkness. The train had passed through Las Vegas and was hurtling on into the night. I was stalling the time of meeting, and not just because of a romantic delusion. Five years can be a long time.

Marty had played in two Broadway shows after she married the director, Kurt Reston. Then she left New York, but I don't know when she settled on the West Coast – or when she changed men again. The new one was named William Dekker and appeared to be some kind of movie mogul. So what had happened to Kurt Reston? There *were* private detectives in California. Why did Marty really want me? Because I was safe? Or she hoped I was? How safe did she need?

Suspicion goes with my work. A cop doesn't meet the most honest people, not even a private cop. Especially a private cop.

Meet the Author:
Dennis Lynds

A raconteur and Renaissance man, Dennis Lynds changed the mystery form and along the way created colorful private detectives who consistently won awards as well as the hearts of readers. He was a tall, lanky man with a nose the size of Gibraltar and a generous nature that made him a soft touch for friends, panhandlers, and his children. He published some 40 novels under various pseudonyms, won awards such as the Edgar, the mystery world's highest honor, and received accolades from legendary authors like Ross Macdonald. "A novelist of power and quality, … one of the major imaginative creators in the crime field," Macdonald wrote of him.

The New York Times named several of Lynds's novels to its Best Mysteries of the Year lists. Remarkably, two of them written under different pseudonyms appeared on the same list – *Silent Scream* by Michael Collins and *Circle of Fire* by Mark Sadler.

Amused, Lynds said that none of the *Times* editors realized he was both Collins and Sadler. "I don't think they ever figured it out," he explained. And he never bothered to tell them.

Seldom does an author change the course of a genre once; rarely twice. Lynds is credited with being the writer who, in the late 1960s and early 1970s, propelled the detective novel into the Modern Age. His most famous pen name was Michael Collins. With that name, he created the opinionated Dan Fortune, the star of one of America's longest-running private detective series. The first book, *Act of Fear*, won the Edgar Allan Poe Award for Best First Novel. "Many critics believe Dan Fortune to be the culmination of a maturing process that transformed the private eye from the naturalistic Spade (Dashiell Hammett) through the romantic Marlowe (Raymond Chandler) and the psychological Archer (Ross Macdonald) to the sociological Fortune," according to *Private Eyes: 101 Knights* by Robert Baker and Michael Nietzel.

At heart, Lynds was a rebel. Two decades later, he rattled mystery critics and changed the field again, this time by introducing literary techniques into the genre, beginning in the late 1980s with *Red Rosa, Castrato*, and *Chasing Eights*, and continuing well into the 1990s with *The Irishman's Horse, Cassandra in Red*, and *The Cadillac Cowboy*. Other authors followed, proving the flexibility and durability of the suspense world. "No one could accuse [Lynds] of reworking the same turf in his novels. ... His last several books have pushed the private-eye form into some fascinating new shapes," according to *The Wall Street Journal* in 2000. *The Los Angeles Times* commented, "It takes style to bring that off. Bravery, too, of course."

Lynds also published mainstream novels, short stories, and poetry. Five of his literary short stories were honored in *Best American Short Stories*.

During World War II, he was a rifleman and carried books of poetry in his knapsack as he fought across France. He was a strong swimmer, so when he and fellow infantrymen were surrounded by Nazis, he plunged into an icy river, leading them to escape. He earned two Purple Hearts and a Bronze Star. Later he graduated with a degree in chemistry from Hofstra and a masters degree in journalism from Syracuse. A lifelong New Yorker, in the mid 1960s he finally left the East Coast's bitter winters to settle in the warm sunshine of Southern California. He was married three times, to Doris Flood, then Sheila McErlean, and finally to Gayle Hallenbeck Stone Lynds. He had two daughters, Katie and Deirdre Lynds, and two step children, Paul and Julia Stone.

Dennis Lynds died at age 81 in 2005. Jack Adrian wrote in *The Financial Times*, "Unusually for a mystery writer – as a breed, they tend to favor things as they are, rather than as they might be – the American author Dennis Lynds, politically, came from left of center. This did not mean he preached bloody revolution. He wrote to entertain." Entertainment was something Lynds never forgot, that and to be generous to his friends.

Obituaries celebrating his work appeared around the globe. In a typical understatement, he commented near the end of his life, "I had a good run." His career had lasted more than fifty years.

The Nightrunners
#9 in the Edgar Award–winning Dan Fortune mystery series
by Dennis Lynds
Originally published under the pseudonym Michael Collins

Wallace Kern was a rich man, president and owner of his father's pharmaceutical company. His brother, William ("Bill") Kern, was just a car salesman and disdained by his ambitious family. But then, Bill was also a compulsive gambler who went on sprees and wrote bad checks to cover his losses. In the no-holds-barred Chelsea district of 1970s New York City where private detective Dan Fortune worked, Bill Kern was known as a paperhanger.

Wallace hires Fortune to drag his gambling brother back home from his latest fling. But Fortune soon discovers the truth: the brother has disappeared with the money he was supposed to use to get Wallace's son out of a Mexican jail. That's a big problem. Followed by a bigger problem: murder.

Here is a gripping story of the iconic detective following the violent twists of a trail that leads him from mansions and glassy skyscraper offices to dark Manhattan rooftops where cop and killer stalk one another. You'll watch backroom card games and meet gamblers, dope-pushers, and killers – the nightrunners – until, finally, and worst of all for Fortune, he has to avenge a personal loss.

"Briskly paced, tersely told." – *The Buffalo Evening News*

"[Lynds] juggles everything around like the expert he is, and the complications are nicely resolved." – *The New York Times*

"A fast-pace thriller … a good book to read at one sitting on a rainy evening." – *Minneapolis Tribune*

"[Lynds] writes with firmness and intelligence. His style is staccato, matched to the action and tone." – *Washington Post*

###

www.ingramcontent.com/pod-product-compliance
Lightning Source LLC
Chambersburg PA
CBHW061154170626
46809CB00003B/1090